HER COWBOY
BILLIONAIRE BLIND DATE

Christmas in Coral Canyon Romance Book 7

LIZ ISAACSON

AEJ
CREATIVE WORKS

ISBN-13: 978-1690634355

CHAPTER 1

A manda Whittaker sighed as she closed the door, turning and letting her eyes flutter shut as she sagged into the wood behind her. She wondered what Ryder was doing on the other side. He'd certainly seemed stunned, and Amanda actually was too.

They'd been out four times now, and she just didn't feel a spark with him. At age sixty-two, she didn't have time to date a man she didn't feel much for, even if she enjoyed spending time with someone besides her poochon. And that wasn't even a someone. The little black poodle bichon frise mix certainly didn't speak English.

She did balance on Amanda's knee and whine, excited her master was home. Amanda bent down and said, "Hey, baby," scooping the little dog into her arms. She moved away from the door as she continued. "I broke up with Ryder tonight. Just now, actually."

Right when he'd leaned in to kiss her.

Another sigh leaked from her mouth.

Maybe I shouldn't have broken up with Jason.

It was not the first time the thought had crossed her mind in the past six months. She'd spent three Christmases with Jason. Two and a half years. He was a good man, and she'd loved him. She believed he loved her. But the man had a serious temper, and he'd lost his son because of some terrible things he'd said and done.

And he was completely unrepentant, and he'd stopped going to church years ago. They'd talked about faith and religion dozens of times, and in the end, he just couldn't come back. Didn't want the same things she did.

Seeing no other choice, she'd ended their relationship. Since then, she'd been lonelier than ever, second only to the months after her husband had died.

She allowed herself to weep as she fed Beans and refilled the little dog's water bowl. She'd curl up in bed and Beans would lay right against her hip, and Amanda would figure out what to do in the morning.

Sunday morning, which she'd spend at church and then she'd go to lunch at Whiskey Mountain Lodge with her sons, their wives, families, and friends.

She wouldn't be alone, and she was infinitely grateful for that.

The following morning, she slipped on her heels and said to Beans, "I'll be back later, Beany Baby," and headed out to her car. At least it was summer, and she didn't have to worry about driving in snow.

Despite living in Wyoming for her entire adult life,

Amanda didn't particularly enjoy winter, and if the snow and wind was bad, she didn't leave the house. After all, she didn't have to. She had no job, no obligations besides those she chose. Visiting friends, or serving people in her church, or helping a neighbor down the street with yard work or baking or making cards for their grandchildren.

She and Ronald had worked hard to provide a good life for their boys, and when he'd died, Amanda and all the children had become billionaires. And yet, money couldn't seem to help find her a man that she wanted to spend the rest of her life with.

She set aside the thoughts as she went into the chapel. Beau and Lily always saved her a spot on the end of the row, and she hated how it was twice as much room as she needed. Of course, she'd been coming to church with Ryder for a week or two now, and she hadn't sent any texts about the break-up.

"I'll take Charlie," she whispered as she sat down, leaving several inches of space between her and her son.

"Hey, Ma," he said, looking behind her. "No Ryder today?"

"We broke up," she said, gesturing for him to hand her the baby. Charlie had just turned eighteen months, and his chubby cheeks and quick smile disguised the fact that he'd spent several weeks in the NICU as a preemie.

"Broke up?" Beau took Charlie from Lily and passed him to Amanda.

She grinned at the baby and kissed him. He was so perfect, and she loved her grandchildren with everything in her. Beau set the diaper bag on the bench between them. "I thought you liked him."

"I did," Amanda said, glancing up to the pulpit and hoping the pastor would start soon so she wouldn't have to answer her son's questions. It wouldn't matter if it was now or later. She'd have to answer them. "I do."

"Did he break up with you?"

"No," she said. "There was just no...connection there."

"Mom," Beau said, his eyes alight with concern.

"I'm fine," she said. "We went out four times."

"You should let me and Graham set you up," he said. "He knows tons of guys, and—"

"I don't want a *guy*," Amanda said, throwing a glare in Beau's direction. "And I don't want to be set up." It wasn't the first time Beau had suggested such a thing. Amanda hadn't had any problems getting her own dates, thank you very much. The problem was, she hadn't had any luck choosing the right men either.

Men, not guys.

She wasn't flirty and thirty, or even forty and fabulous. Heck, fifty was in her rear-view mirror.

The sermon started, and Beau focused his attention up front—or on Lily. She wasn't sure which, but Amanda didn't mind. She got to cuddle with her grandson and feed him crackers and listen to the pastor talk about treating everyone with respect.

About halfway through the sermon, her phone buzzed in her purse, and she pulled it out. Graham, her oldest son, had texted. *No Ryder today? Beau says you broke up.*

Amanda rolled her eyes, sure Graham would somehow be able to feel it. And she wasn't dignifying his text with a response. He didn't need one. Ryder's absence on the bench was confirmation enough.

"Stop texting your brother," she hissed to Beau, who simply smiled at her and then looked back up to the dais. She didn't hear much of the sermon after that, and she took Charlie with her out into the lobby.

His other grandma waited there, with his grandpa, and she passed the baby to Jack Everett with a smile. "Do you want to ride up to the lodge with us?" Fran asked, taking the diaper bag from Amanda.

"I think I'm going to go with Vi today," she said, looking around. "She wanted me to talk to her about making a coconut cream pie for Todd's birthday."

Sure enough, one of the blonde Everett sisters came out of the chapel with her arm through her husband's. She brushed her short hair back and asked, "Amanda, you're coming with us, right?"

"Yep." Vi and Todd lived in town, so they'd be coming back this way later, and Amanda rode up to the lodge with them often. Or another of the Everetts, as it made no sense for so many to drive up the canyon only to drive back down.

Beau and Lily appeared, and Amanda was suddenly anxious to leave. She didn't want to get bombarded with more break-up questions, and she inched toward the door. But Graham exited the chapel on the other side and made a beeline for her before she could get very far.

He carried little Ronnie in his arms, and he said, "Mom, I know just the guy for you."

"Man," Beau said, nudging Graham. "He knows just the *man* for you, Mom."

She looked back and forth between her sons, her patience so thin with them already. Perhaps she should just go home today. Heat up some leftovers. Snuggle with Beans and a pot of coffee.

Beau and Graham looked at her with bright eyes filled with hope, and Amanda wanted to give them the world, same as she always had.

She sighed, knowing she was about to regret the words that came out of her mouth.

"Fine," she said. "Set it up."

❦

A WEEK LATER, Amanda had tried everything in her power to get out of the blind date Graham had arranged for her. He wouldn't even tell her the name of the man he knew, and Amanda was beginning to think he didn't know anyone.

But hey, she hadn't heard the word *guy* again. It was always, *Mom, I promise you'll like this man,* or *Mom, this man is perfect for you.*

After her son's texts, maybe she was hopeful. She also knew how dangerous hope could be, and she tried not to hold onto it too tightly.

She knew there were apps for older singles like her, but

she wasn't ready to go there yet. She really just wanted a calm man. One with good values and morals. One who could support himself. Who just needed someone to talk to at night, the way she did. One ready to love, even if it only lasted for a few years.

"That was Jason's problem," she murmured as she put her earrings on. "He wasn't ready to let go of the past and love."

She'd told Graham and Beau very early on *No cowboys. No one in their forties.*

That had sparked one of Graham's most disturbing messages from that week.

How young can I go?

Jason had been ten years younger than her, so she said fifty-two, and then begged Graham to tell her who he was thinking of setting her up with.

He'd done no such thing, and she was meeting this mystery man at Devil's Tower in thirty minutes, just as Beau had directed her. He'd also said *Mom, every man in Wyoming is a cowboy. How non-cowboy are we talking?*

She hadn't answered, because a few minutes later, Graham had given more details about the date. She was supposed to wear her silver scarf, which was ridiculous this close to June, but that was what her son had said.

Between the two of them badgering her, Amanda had decided to just roll with it. Wear what they said to wear. Be where they said to be.

She draped the silver scarf over her blue sweater, and

the two colors really worked with her dark hair salted with gray and her dark blue eyes.

That squirrel of hope moved through her again, and she took a deep breath to contain the giddy feeling in her stomach she got whenever she went out with a new man. There was always such an excitement, even if she didn't know who he was.

Twenty-eight minutes later, she pulled into Devil's Tower and clicked across the parking lot to the front doors. She wasn't an idiot, and she'd seen Beau's truck in the back of the lot, almost like he'd been trying to hide it.

She didn't see him inside, nor Graham, and she gave her name to the hostess. "Right this way, Mrs. Whittaker," the girl said, despite there being several couples obviously waiting for a table.

She was seated in a booth over on the side, away from the doors but with a good view of the park across the street from the restaurant. Nerves hit her then, and she wondered how long she'd have to wait.

"Something to drink?" a man asked, easily thirty or forty years younger than Amanda.

She gave him a kind smile and said, "Yes, please. I'll have a frozen raspberry lemonade."

The young man left, and she casually looked at the menu, noting that the hostess had put down a second one across from her, as if she knew Amanda would be meeting someone.

A few minutes later, the waiter put her lemonade down

and said, "I'll be right back, ma'am," leaving her with the bright pink concoction.

She ripped the wrapper off the straw and swirled it through the drink before taking a sip. It was perfectly sour and sweet and delicious, and she sighed. Maybe this blind date wouldn't be so bad.

Please let this be the one, she prayed. She picked up her glass again, the chill of it against her fingers reminding her to take a deep breath. Everything would be okay. But she'd never had this much trouble finding someone she liked. She'd married her husband when she was only eighteen, and after only a few months of dating.

"Amanda?" a man asked.

She swung her head toward the man standing at the end of the table. He didn't look like a cowboy, thank goodness.

She didn't know him, but he was tall, with sandy hair and the brightest pair of blue eyes she'd ever seen. They sparkled at her, and she lost the words that had been in her mind.

"I'm Finley Barber," he said, extending his hand for her to shake. "I think you're my date for the night. Silver scarf." He grinned, and Amanda's pulse went nuts. He was handsome, and she wondered where in the world Graham and Beau had found him.

She stuck her hand out, realizing a moment too late that she was holding that raspberry lemonade.

Horror struck her as the thick, red liquid went flying, hitting the gorgeous man right in the abdomen.

CHAPTER 2

Things had been moving in slow motion for Finley Barber. His truck wouldn't seem to go over forty miles per hour the whole way from Dog Valley. His feet seemed to be going backward as he walked into Devil's Tower.

And getting to the table with the pretty woman wearing the silver scarf? It had taken a year.

As soon as that ice cold drink hit his skin, though, everything rushed forward. Before he knew it, Amanda had scooted out of the booth. "I'm so sorry," she said, grabbing her napkin and pressing it against his stomach.

Everyone in the vicinity was looking at them, and Finn tried to smile. But wow, that stuff was *cold*.

"It's fine," he said, taking the napkin and stepping back. "Really."

A waiter appeared, and he handed Finn his black towel. "I'll get you another drink, ma'am." Another man appeared, and he swept away the tipped glass and all the liquid in the blink of an eye.

"Would you like something to drink?" the waiter asked, and Finn blinked, trying to get all the pieces aligned in his head.

"I'll bring some water," the waiter said, and he left Finn and Amanda alone. She let out a shaky laugh and wiped her palms down the front of her thighs.

"I'm so sorry," she said again. "I don't know what I was thinking."

He wiped the slush off his shirt and said, "It's just a polo. I own a washing machine." He gestured to the bench where she'd been sitting. "Please. Sit down."

She did, which allowed Finn to do the same. He left the towel at the end of the table and looked at Amanda. She had beautiful eyes, dark like the blue depths of the ocean. Her shoulder-length hair held swirls of gray, and he really liked that she didn't try to cover them up. Hide them underneath dyes and chemicals.

"So you're Graham's mother," he said, adding a smile to it. He could clearly see the shape of Graham's nose in Amanda, as well as feel it in the energy she put off.

"That's right," she said. "I'm Amanda Whittaker."

"He didn't tell me I'd be meeting his mother." Finn wasn't sure what he'd have done differently. *Maybe said no,* he thought. After all, he valued his friendship with Graham and Laney, and if his mother didn't like him, would that be broken?

"Yes, well, he didn't tell me anything either," Amanda

said, glancing up when the waiter set down a fresh slushy drink.

"Have you had a chance to look at our drink menu?" he asked.

Finn had not, but he said, "Bring me one of those too, would you please?"

"Sure thing."

"It's frozen raspberry lemonade," Amanda said as the waiter walked away.

"Sounds great," Finn said. He leaned closer like he was about to share a very deep secret. "I haven't been on a date in a while. I'm pretty rusty."

"Oh, that's okay," Amanda said, sticking her straw in her slush. "I've been out loads of times." Her eyes widened. "I mean—I—my husband died six years ago, and I've dated a few men since then."

Finn nodded. "I know about Graham's father."

"Do you have children?" she asked. The silver-haired dating scene had plenty of divorces, widows, and children —grandchildren even. Not that Finn would know. He spent the majority of his time with equines, dogs, and chickens.

Amanda did not seem like the kind of woman to appreciate any of those things, and he wished his heart wasn't beating so fast. She was mighty pretty though, and Finn hadn't been out with anyone in a couple of years. Not since Kristen had stuck around long enough for him to fall in love with her, only to find out she was really interested in his bank account and not being his wife.

"Finley?" she asked.

"Finn," he said. "I go by Finn. Two N's."

She smiled again and took a sip of her drink. "Okay, Finn. Do you have children?"

"Yes," he said, getting his brain to work. "I've got two daughters. Joann is thirty, and Kimberly is twenty-seven. They live in Jackson Hole. My ex-wife lives there too."

She nodded, absorbing the information without a trace of judgement on her face. Finn appreciated that. "And where do you live? I think I'd know if you were here in Coral Canyon."

"Would you?" he asked, grinning at her. "How's that?"

"Well, I've lived here for almost forty-five years. This place isn't that big."

"It's gotten a lot bigger recently," he said, glancing out the window as if the evidence of town growth would be right there.

"True," Amanda said. "But I still think I'd know if there was a handsome man like you in town. Available."

His gaze flew back to hers. *Handsome?* She really was better at this dating thing than he was. "I live in Dog Valley," he said. "I own a boarding stable out there." She didn't need to know that he came from one of the richest racehorse stables in the country. Or that, years ago, he'd invented the software she probably used to do her online banking. Or that the horses he bred, trained, and worked with sold for hundreds of thousands of dollars.

No one needed to know that. At least not right now.

"Dog Valley," she said, that smile showing all her straight, white teeth. "That's great."

"Yeah?" he asked. "It's thirty minutes away from here."

"Less staring," she said with a definite hint of flirtation in her voice.

Finn laughed, wishing he'd worn his cowboy hat. Graham had warned him against it though, saying the woman he was meeting needed to be "eased in" to the idea of dating a cowboy.

Finn had almost called it off right then. He *was* a cowboy. He'd been born with spurs on. Dust for blood. The sound of horse's hooves clomping in his nursery at night.

"Oh, I think you'll find plenty of people staring in Dog Valley," he said. "Remember how I said I hadn't been out with anyone in a while?" He shook his head, glad when his frozen drink came too, and he had something else to focus on.

"People know you then?" she asked.

"Yes," he said simply. "People out there know me."

She kept the smile in place, and Finn let her ask another question, hoping he could live up the standards of this woman, get her number for himself, and set up a second date real soon.

"AND SHE HAS GRANDKIDS," he told Vanilla, the yellow lab who followed him everywhere. Chocolate and

Licorice had gotten sick of the date recap about ten minutes ago, but Finn was still floating on air.

He'd just gone on a date for the first time in two years, and it wasn't horrible. In fact, it was downright amazing, and he had left Devil's Tower with Amanda's number in his phone and the promise to call her dripping from his lips.

"She's a little older than me," he told Vanilla as he shut off all the lights and made sure the doors were locked. He had three Labrador retrievers, and they'd definitely alert him if there was a problem. Not that Finn expected any. His land was pretty remote, with the nearest neighbor living five miles away.

But sometimes wild animals ventured onto his property, scaring the horses. He made sure they were all locked properly in the barn each night, because losing one was like losing an entire year's salary.

"I just can't believe we hit it off," he said. "I honestly wasn't expecting to like her. I was only doing it as a favor to Graham." When his friend had called and said he had the perfect date for Finn, he'd almost said no.

But something in him had made him pause and listen. "He still should've said it was his mother, don't you think?"

Vanilla didn't answer, just clicked alongside Finn as he went down the hall to the master suite. Chocolate and Licorice were curled up on the right side of the bed, practically on top of one another. Vanilla jumped up there next to them, circled around, and flopped down.

"You guys will have to move so I can get the covers," he said, their nightly routine. Of course, the dogs would not move. They were three of the most stubborn canines on the planet, almost like they prided themselves on being wonderful, loyal, and downright maddening.

If Finn had a bit of liver pinched between his fingers, all three of them would do whatever he said. And they were great with the horses, and Licorice could even herd the chickens.

"Go on," he said. "Move." He had to heave the dogs off the bed one by one to get his blanket out from under them, and then he fell asleep almost instantly, a smile on his face for the first time in a long, long time.

The following morning, Finn forced himself to work through his morning chores as normal. Set a pot of coffee to brew as normal. Set bread in the toaster. Take his vitamins. Send a couple of texts to his daughters.

It was Sunday, so he showered and as he walked down the hall, adjusting his tie, he decided he'd waited long enough to call Amanda.

Weren't men supposed to call the next day?

He wasn't sure what time she'd be at church, though they had talked about her pastor a bit the night before. Well, she had. Amanda had pretty much dominated the conversation as Finn loosened up and remembered what it was like to talk to a beautiful woman.

He hadn't been great at it, but he felt he could improve, with enough time and practice. He felt younger than he had in years as the phone rang. He fiddled with his knot still, something about it not right. But he couldn't devote full brain power to fixing it, because he was calling Amanda Whittaker.

His heart raced faster with every second she didn't pick up. The call finally ended, and he hung up before her voicemail message started.

A moment later, his phone buzzed in his hand, cutting through the disappointment raging through him. *In church,* Amanda said. *I'll call you later?*

Mine starts in a half an hour, he messaged back, his thumbs feeling thick and slow.

Maybe I could bring you lunch, she said, and Finn's breath burst from his body.

Sure, his sausage-fingers typed out. *Not spending today with your family?*

She'd mentioned the lodge up the west canyon, and when she spoke of her sons, their wives and families, it was clear she loved them deeply. Finn had liked that. Liked the enthusiasm family sparked in her.

He didn't see his daughters much, and he had no reason to talk to Holly anymore. But he loved Kimberly and Joann, and he did talk to them, text them, and stay in touch with them regularly. Neither of them was interested in breeding and training racehorses, but Finn hadn't been able to give up his boarding stable, tuck his tail, and return to Nashville.

He wouldn't.

He didn't need his father's power and prestige. He was

doing just fine selling to the rich and famous on his own. Of course, his last name helped.

It had been too long for him to return to the family farms in Nashville anyway. He'd been gone for thirty-five years, and grudges ran deep in the South.

Amanda hadn't answered his question, and he would be late for church if he didn't get going. So he banished thoughts of his father to the back of his mind, took off his tie and re-tied it, and headed out the door, hoping he hadn't upset Amanda by asking her about her family.

After all, he really had no idea how to date at age fifty-five, with a bruised heart and his whole life wrapped up in horses that ate better meals than he did.

CHAPTER 3

Amanda kept her phone face-down on her lap, though she'd felt the buzz from a text several minutes ago. Beau had been watching her like a hawk since she'd arrived, and Graham had deviated from his usual spot in the chapel.

She'd arrived late on purpose, barely sliding onto the end of the bench just as Pastor Franklin had stood up to begin. Lily hadn't handed over Charlie, and Amanda's tension hadn't eased a single bit—until Finn had called.

Beau had seen the screen, and then he'd focused on his own phone. The sneak. She didn't need her sons gossiping about her love life, though she didn't really have one of those.

Finally, the sermon ended, and she exploded to her feet only to find Andrew standing there, blocking her escape. He was just as tall and wide as his brothers, and Amanda sighed. Out of all of her sons, Andrew had had the hardest time with her dating after his father had died.

That was a few years ago, though, and he handed his daughter Chrissy to her and said, "Want to ride up to the lodge with me and Becca today?"

"I'm not going to the lodge today," Amanda said, deciding on the spot.

"Her date went really well last night," Beau said, sandwiching her on the other side.

"How do you know?" she asked, shaking her head even as a smile crossed her face.

"He called you, and you lit up like the Christmas tree at the lodge." Beau chuckled and nudged her farther out into the aisle so he and Lily could get out too. "Here comes Graham."

"So, Mom," he said, somehow shouldering his way into the aisle beside Andrew. "How did you like Finn?"

She looked around at her three sons, wishing Eli was there with them. A sudden, powerful pang of missing hit her. For her son and his wife and family in California. For her husband.

Though it had been six years, tears still pricked her eyes that she couldn't go home to him. Smile, and ask him about work. Put something in the oven and talk about church. She'd loved him so much, and she could see parts of him in each of her son's faces as they looked at her, waiting for an explanation.

She drew in a deep breath. "He was great," she admitted. "I really liked him."

A smile burst across Graham's face. "That's great, Mom."

"She's not coming to the lodge," Andrew said.

"She offered to take him lunch," Beau added.

"Okay, I'm leaving." Amanda handed Chrissy back to Andrew, and the little girl started fussing and reaching for Amanda again. So she took her back, absolute love flowing through her as the two-year-old hugged her.

"Are you really taking him lunch?" Graham asked.

"I don't even know how you saw that," Amanda said, glaring at Beau.

"I have good eyes. What can I say?"

"I told him not to spy on you," Lily said. "He—"

"We just want you to be happy," Beau said over his wife. "So go. Make something delicious for lunch. We'll miss you at the lodge." He leaned over and kissed his mother on the forehead.

Graham did too, and Andrew took his daughter back and hugged Amanda. "Have fun, Mom."

She watched them walk away from her, the chapel nearly empty now. Part of her mourned the fact that she wouldn't be spending the afternoon with them. And the other part of her couldn't wait to get home and start leafing through her recipe book.

TWO HOURS LATER, she had Finn's address in her phone, a pot of chicken tortilla soup in a box on the passenger seat beside her, and her nerves bouncing around like jumping beans.

And Beans on her lap, comforting her. She'd texted Finn several times as she waited for the soup to simmer to perfection, and he'd said to bring out her dog. *Plenty of animals out here,* he said. *I have three dogs.*

Three dogs.

Amanda had asked what kind, and he'd told her they were all Labradors. "Big dogs," she said to Beans. "Don't let them scare you, okay, baby?"

She turned when her maps program told her to, and the road turned from asphalt to dirt. A couple of miles down the road, the buildings started. And not cheap ones. Really nice, well-kept buildings in an array of sizes.

"Wow," she said. Finn had never said what he did for a living, but she saw the *Barber's Racehorses and Breeds* sign painted in huge letters on the side of building that had to be a hundred yards long.

The house sat just past that, as per his instructions, and she pulled in beside a big, navy blue truck with a round logo on the driver's door. Amanda looked at the house, and it felt...nice. Homey. Like a place that had a feminine hand guiding it, though Finn had said he hadn't dated in a while.

She got out and rounded the front of her SUV as Finn came down the front steps. "Hey," he said, a smile on his face and in his voice. "Can I help?"

"Sure." She took a moment to look at him. Really look. He was fifty-five-years-old, and absolutely stunning, the

sunlight haloing him in golden rays. "Hey." Without
thinking too hard, she stepped over to him and put one
hand on his shoulder. Tipping up to his height, she kissed
his cheek. "It's good to see you. How was church?"

She moved away, so many sensations prickling through
her. He smelled good, and looked dashing in those dark
slacks, white shirt, and striped tie. She'd always liked a
man in a tie, and wow, he wore his well.

"Good," he said behind her, his voice a bit lower than
normal. She glanced over her shoulder to find he hadn't
moved.

"Come grab these rolls, would you?" She opened the
door and reached for the bag of rolls she'd bought on the
way out. "I can't wait to try your peach jam."

That set him into motion, and he took the bread from
her. "I hope you like it. It's my sister's recipe."

Amanda heaved the pot out of the box and kicked the
door closed with her foot. She'd changed out of her dress
for church, and she suddenly felt self-conscious as she
followed Finn up the sidewalk to the front door.

"This is a beautiful place," she said, taking in the
emerald green grass, the flowers lining the cement, the
huge pot of petunias on the porch. Windchimes tinkled
from the rain gutter, and he even had a red, white, and
blue wreath hanging on the front door.

Amanda didn't know what to think, but she sure did
like the peaceful feeling of this house, this land, this man.

Feeling a bit out of sorts, she followed him inside.
Three dogs immediately started sniffing her, one black,

one yellow, and one brown. "Oh, Beans," she said, remembering her poochon in the car.

"I'll get her." Finn set the rolls on the kitchen counter and turned back toward her. He paused right at her side and looked at her. "It's good to see you, too."

Warmth filled her whole body as his footsteps went back out the front door. A smile touched her lips, and she set the pot on the stove though it was probably still plenty warm. She could turn on a burner, and she did, listening to the clicking of the gas until the flame caught.

She turned and looked around the kitchen, dining room, and living area, the wide windows along the back wall showing a large deck and yard and barns beyond.

In that moment, she realized that Finn was very, very wealthy. He'd said nothing about it at dinner the night before. In fact, he'd said very little about himself. He'd talked about his family, his daughters, and Dog Valley. His dogs and horses.

But not much about himself.

"That's because you dominated the conversation," she muttered to herself, stepping over to the double doors that led outside.

A moment later, a shrill, sharp bark filled the air, and she turned back to find Beans cowering among the bigger dogs. "It's okay, Beany Baby," she said, crossing over to the scene just inside the front door. Beans had a small dog personality, with loads of nervous energy that usually wore off within a few minutes.

She sniffed and let herself be sniffed, and Finn smiled

at the dogs as he slipped his hand into Amanda's. She stilled and looked down at their now joined hands. His skin was warm and wonderful, and she felt like a young woman again, standing there with her brand-new boyfriend, the possibilities before them endless.

"I made chicken tortilla soup," she said. "I know it's almost June, but I'm of the opinion that soup can be consumed any time of year." She flashed him a smile, and he chuckled. She tugged on his hand, and they walked into the kitchen together.

"So, Finn," she said, dropping his hand and opening a drawer in the hopes of finding a ladle. "What do you do for a living?"

He didn't answer right away, and Amanda continued in her quest to find the utensils she wanted. She did, turning her back to him to stir the soup.

"I breed and sell racehorses," he finally said.

"I saw the sign on the barn on the way in."

"That was my arena," he said, clearing his throat afterward.

Amanda appreciated the nerves she heard in his voice. She kept her eyes on the food, hoping this wasn't too sensitive of a subject. "Do you maintain everything yourself?"

"Yes, ma'am. I mean, I have a few guys come in sometimes. During harvest season. Springtime to get everything up for the summer. That kind of stuff."

Amanda glanced at him, her feelings for him too soft already. She'd fallen fast for Ronald when she was younger, but she'd been much more careful with her heart in the past several years.

Until Finn. She felt herself sliding right down a slippery slope already, and she'd been out with him one time. Hadn't even known him for twenty-four hours yet.

"How'd you get into racehorses?"

"Uh, my father bred them. In Kentucky."

Amanda abandoned the soup now, turning toward him instead. He stood at the counter, pulling knives and spoons out of a drawer in the island. He turned and opened a cupboard to pull down a couple of bowls, and their eyes met.

"If I looked you up on the Internet...." Amanda let the question hang there.

"Oh, well." He shrugged and continued getting the dishes out. "You'd find a lot about my father. The Barber horse farms are some of the biggest in the South."

"Ah, I see." She turned off the flame beneath the soup. "I think this is ready."

CHAPTER 4

Finn's heart seemed to be connected to an extra fifty amps of power whenever he looked at Amanda. Thought about Amanda. And a man his age needed to be careful with his heart.

He set the dishes on the counter and faced her. "Might as well say this right now. I have a lot of money." He didn't want to push her away, not right when they were just starting out. But he figured he might as well be honest with her.

"My last girlfriend cared more about the bank account than me." Wow, the words burned his throat, more than he thought they should after all this time.

"I have my own bank account," Amanda said coolly. "I'm really sorry that happened to you."

All the tension in the house seemed to leak right out of the roof, and Finn smiled. "Thank you. I happen to think soup is an acceptable meal any time of year, too."

Amanda blinked, and then she burst out laughing, and it had been a long time since Finn had experienced that level of happiness at such a simple thing.

Amanda ran out to her car to get the tortilla strips, and Finn watched the four dogs play together in the living room. "This is crazy, right?" he whispered to himself, not really expecting anyone to answer.

He tipped his head back and looked at the ceiling, through it, hoping to gaze right into heaven itself. "Please guide me," he prayed, not sure how to ask for more than that when it came to Amanda.

The sermon that day had been about loving others, and Finn had enjoyed the choir numbers, the flow of people around him, and the idea that he wouldn't be spending Sunday alone.

Amanda returned, and she bustled around his kitchen as easily as if she lived there. She served the soup with a smile, and Finn couldn't help smiling back. He really liked her presence here, and he wondered how far he'd go to keep her with him.

Would she even consider moving to Dog Valley? Surely she had a nice place in Coral Canyon too.

Thinking way too far down the line, he told himself, picking up a spoon. "So tell me," he said. "What do you spend your time doing?"

"Oh, a little of this and a little of that," she said airily. Finn detected a hint of falseness in her voice, but she ducked her head, that dark hair falling between them. He wasn't sure how to press her on the subject if she didn't want to talk about it, and she moved the conversation to something else before he could figure it out.

She talked about her boys—who were all grown men now. In fact, Finn was only a dozen years older than Graham—and her home. She talked about her husband's energy company, and Finn filled her in on his brief marriage and divorce.

"I'm sorry it didn't work out," Amanda said, the sky starting to darken. They'd been sitting on the back porch since lunchtime, and Finn needed to get out and check on all his animals.

"It's okay," Finn said, standing up. "You want to walk around the farm a bit? I need to go check on the horses. Bring them in for the night."

A blip of apprehension crossed her pretty face, and she ran her hands up her arms. "I don't think so. I should get on home." She smiled at him. "I didn't talk too much today, did I?" She looked really worried about it, and Finn wanted to erase that from her face. From her whole life.

"You talked a normal amount today," he said.

"It's just that I know I talked too much last night, and I didn't want to do that today."

Finn felt like he'd told her just about everything about him. At least all the surface things. The things she'd find on the Internet if she went looking. But he didn't think she would.

"I enjoyed last night and today," he said, moving back over to her. "Thanks for driving all the way out here." She smiled as he approached, and he brushed his lips along her temple. "I'll see you later, okay?"

"Okay."

He whistled and the dogs perked up from where they'd settled in the shade of the trees in the backyard. "C'mon, boys," he said to them. "Time to get to work."

Beans ran up the steps, and Amanda scooped the little dog into her arms. He'd already carried everything of hers out to her luxury SUV, and she waved one last time before he turned and walked down the steps.

He told himself not to look back. Not even once. And he didn't.

In the gathering darkness, he fed the chickens and gathered in all the horses from their pastures. All but the two most stubborn ones stood at the doors already, giving him a look like *Where have you been?*

"Sorry, guys," he said to them. "There was a woman here. Did you hear her laughing?" Finn couldn't get over the fact that Amanda had come to Dog Valley to feed him lunch.

At the same time, Finn felt a resistance in himself he didn't understand. He'd never been one to fall in love quickly, and in fact, he'd only loved a couple of other women in the past. He knew Amanda had her own bank account, and that was a relief.

So he put his head down and got the work done, returning to the house by the light of the flashlight on his phone. Inside, he realized he'd missed several texts, and it seemed like the whole Whittaker family had decided to text him while he took care of the essentials on the farm. Tomorrow, he'd have a couple of extra hours of work that he hadn't done that night, but everyone was fed and watered, and that was all that mattered.

His house felt emptier than it had in a long while, and he tried to ignore it as he read Graham's texts.

How's it going with my mom? I told you I had someone perfect for you.

The pressure of dating one of his friend's mother's smothered Finn, and he didn't know how to answer. He didn't normally kiss and tell, or talk about his relationships, period. But he'd be seeing Graham and Laney tomorrow, as he went to pick up feed for his chickens and a couple of saddles she'd custom-made for him.

I'll see you tomorrow, Finn texted to his friend, unsure of what he'd say in person. It felt awkward, and once again, Finn had the distinct feeling that if he'd known the blind date would've been with Graham's mother, he'd have said no.

Beau had also texted, wondering if his mother was still out there or not. He'd texted three times, the last one saying, *Never mind. I got in touch with her. Sorry, Finn.*

He wasn't sure why Beau was apologizing, and foolishness rushed through Finn. Amanda's boys clearly loved her and relied on her, and he felt guilty taking her from them for the whole afternoon. She'd never said anything about spending time with him over them, but he could put two and two together.

He'd used Beau's brains and lawyer services to incorporate his stables years ago, and they'd stayed in touch since. He'd watched the other man fall in love, retreat to Whiskey Mountain Lodge, and then meet someone else. Fall in love again. Get married and have a baby. It had been Beau that had introduced Finn to Graham and Laney, and he liked those Whittaker men.

And their mother.

He shook his head, trying to get the thoughts out of it. Life was much simpler when he was just feeding horses and throwing a ball for his dogs. He liked weeding the flowerbeds and pruning the roses. He enjoyed clipping the grass and training horses and checking on the hay in the fields.

There was always work to do, which was just fine with Finn. He certainly didn't like being idle, and he'd found a way to fill his life with good things.

Too bad he still felt empty most of the time.

And Amanda had changed that. In one twenty-four-hour period, she'd changed all of that.

"Go slow," he told himself as he closed the door behind Chocolate. "Be careful." He needed to warn himself so he didn't end up with another broken heart.

Amanda had also texted, and she'd said, *I had a great time today.*

Nothing else.

Finn knew how to respond to that. *Me too,* he typed out with a smile on his face. All three dogs jumped up on the bed, circled and flopped, and Finn didn't even tell them to move so he could get the blanket where he liked it.

He just lay down on top of it and gazed up at the ceiling. "Am I doing the right thing?" he asked the Lord, and he waited for an answer.

God had never spoken to him very loudly, and Finn had to listen very carefully to find the answers he needed. He hadn't always done that, and he'd made some serious errors in the past because of it.

Like breaking up his marriage.

He couldn't believe the guilt was still there, but it was. Decades later. Holly had moved on. Gotten remarried. He had a good relationship with her and his daughters now. But there had been a few years where he wondered if he'd have to spend a lifetime paying for some decisions. And he'd vowed he would never make another major life decision—like dating a pretty woman and falling in love with her—without listening to the Lord.

Tonight, nothing came, and he closed his eyes and let his breathing even out. Finally, he thought, *Call Joann.*

He mentally added making a phone call to his oldest daughter to tomorrow's to-do list and drifted off to sleep with gratitude—and maybe a little trepidation about what Joann would say—in his heart.

CHAPTER 5

Amanda had an odd combination of frustration, guilt, and appreciation swimming in her. She'd stayed entirely too long at Finn's, and she knew it.

And now Beau knew it too.

"I'm not sure," she said, making the turn to leave Dog Valley in her rear-view mirror and head back to Coral Canyon. "Is he throwing up?"

"No," Beau said, his son still crying in the background. "He just won't stop crying."

"Well, that's not normal," Amanda said. "Maybe you should bring him down to the emergency room."

"Lily's on the phone with Liam."

"Great," Amanda said, wondering why Beau had called her four times in the space of five minutes over a crying child. But she'd always been there for her sons, and she wanted that now too. None of her other boyfriends had distracted her from being their mother, and Finn couldn't either.

He hadn't. In fact, he wasn't even her boyfriend. They'd seen each other twice and texted back and forth a little bit.

In her heart, she knew it was more than a little bit, but she didn't have to admit it out loud. At least not yet.

"We are going to the ER," Beau said. "Are you on your way back from Dog Valley?"

"Yes," she said. "Do you want me to meet you there?"

"Liam's going to meet us at the clinic," he said, saying something to his wife in a quieter voice. "I'll call you later, Mom." Beau hung up before Amanda could say another word, and that frustration washed over her other emotions.

Her sons had become so needy lately. Or maybe she just felt like they were more involved in her personal life than they'd ever been. "I knew this blind date was a mistake." She shook her head at the landscape around her and reached for her phone. It was almost dead, and if she had car trouble on this lonely stretch of road, she'd need to call for help.

Finn was everything she wanted in a man—except for one major thing. He was a cowboy, and Amanda was not a fan of cowboys.

She'd never said a word to her sons about it, as they all swaggered around town in their cowboy hats and boots. Graham had especially taken to the ranch lifestyle, and most of his belt buckles were bigger than his head.

Beau had gone more mountain man, with his full beard and mustache and letting his hair grow out. Lily had tamed him somewhat, but he still looked like a great big teddy bear cowboy.

Andrew was the most clean-cut because of his job at Springside Energy, her husband's company. But he still wore his cowboy hat when he wasn't working, and he and Becca had signed up for horseback riding lessons at the Buttars Stables. Even Chrissy rode, and Amanda could see them all becoming more and more country as the months passed.

Which was fine. She'd come from the city when she'd married Ron and she'd never regretted it. Not even for a moment. Okay, fine, maybe in the middle of January, there were times she wished she still lived in Dallas.

"Destined for a cowboy," she muttered to herself as her phone rang again. Graham's name sat on the screen this time, and Amanda tapped the console in front of her to connect the Bluetooth to her speakers.

"Hey, Mom," he said.

"Hiya, baby," she said, falling back to her Texas roots. It was warmer there than in Wyoming, but maybe she was destined for a cowboy romance. She'd met Ronald Whittaker the month she'd graduated high school, and he'd whisked her off to the mountains of Wyoming a mere six months later. He was older than her, had already finished college, and had a job at an oil company just outside of Jackson Hole.

"Are you listening to me?" Graham asked, and Amanda blinked at the darkness in front of her.

"No, sorry."

"Ah, so you and Finn are getting along great."

"I barely know the man," Amanda said, having defended herself several times over the years, usually to Andrew, about the men she dated. "I'm old. We do everything slow."

Graham laughed, but it was short-lived. "Also," Amanda said. "Which part of *no cowboys* did you not understand?"

"I didn't get that memo," he said coolly. "You must've told Beau that."

"No," she said, practically yelling the word. "I know I told both of you."

"He wasn't wearing a hat at dinner, was he?" Graham asked, as if he'd planned this conversation.

"No," Amanda said through her teeth, though she wasn't really mad.

"And what about today? Was he wearing a cowboy hat?"

"No."

"Cowboy boots?"

"No, but—"

"Did he have antlers hanging in his house?"

Amanda laughed, finally conceding the point to Graham. "No, but Graham. That man is as cowboy as they come. He's from a racehorse family."

"And we don't like racehorses?" Graham asked. "Because I definitely did not get *that* memo."

Amanda sighed. "I don't know what I don't like."

"So we don't like Finn."

"Would you stop saying we?" Amanda asked. "Last time I checked, you weren't there this afternoon." And that was a very good thing, as she'd held Finn's hand and flirted with him shamelessly. She was definitely interested in him, and for some reason that rubbed her the wrong way.

"Mom, what don't you like about him?" Graham was all business now, the concern in his voice nice to hear for a mother.

"I don't know."

Her son let a few seconds of silence go by, and then he said, "Why don't you swing up to the ranch? Laney and Bailey made cookies and cream ice cream tonight, and there's tons of leftovers."

"I don't think so," Amanda said, feeling tired way down in her bones. "I'll come up tomorrow night and have some. I'm tired."

"Okay," he said. "But, Mom, you'd tell me to figure out what I didn't like or what I wanted, and do something about it."

"Yeah," she said, her thoughts drifting again. "Thanks, sweetie." She hung up, her fingers returning to the wheel to grip it tightly.

What didn't she like about Finn?

He was too much like Ronald.

The idea sat there, swirling softly at first. Then it became a living, breathing thing, completely consuming her mind.

She didn't want another rich cowboy husband. She'd had one of those. Yes, she'd been happy, but she'd learned early in her marriage to make her own way. Do what she wanted. Cook dinner for her and the kids. Ron didn't come home on time for years, and Amanda had learned how to make her own happiness. Just her and the boys.

And that was all she had left.

She had no idea what it took to train a racehorse, but she was betting Finn couldn't spend every afternoon and evening on the deck with her. She hadn't wanted to go out onto his farm with him, because she didn't particularly like animals bigger than her—or chickens—and she didn't want him to know of her distaste for them.

"Maybe this isn't going to be a match," she admitted to herself as she pulled into her driveway. She disliked the defeated tone of her voice—and the figure rising from the front steps. The motion of her car activated the lights, and the front of the house was suddenly bathed in white lights that told her exactly who was waiting for her.

"Ryder." She parked in the garage and got out of the SUV, her heart firing an extra beat every other second. "Hey," she said, rounding the corner toward the front of the house. "What are you doing here?"

"I don't want to break up," he said, swiping his hand through his hair. "And I just thought...I don't know. I thought we could talk."

He approached her, his dark eyes catching the light and reflecting it back to her. He looked apprehensive and thoughtful, qualities she normally admired. Amanda found him handsome with all his dark hair and that scruffy beard.

But as she stood there and let him take her hand in his, she knew they couldn't get back together.

"Ryder," she said with a sigh. "I'm—I just—nothing's changed." She squeezed his fingers. "When you hold my hand, it's just...I don't feel a spark there."

And wow, there had been a whole fireworks show with Finn. Her heart rate accelerated just thinking about him.

"I feel a spark, though," Ryder said.

Amanda didn't want to be cruel. She felt like she'd already been blunt and somewhat unkind as it was. She gently removed her hand from his and backtracked to the car to let Beans out. "Go to the door," she told the dog, following her up the steps and opening the back door for the pup to run inside.

She turned to find Ryder holding the pot of leftover soup. "How are things at Whiskey Mountain Lodge?" he asked.

Amanda blocked him from coming up the steps. "Ryder," she said firmly as she took the pot from him. "You're not coming inside. We're not going to get back together."

His dark eyes stormed at her. "Why not?"

Had he not heard her a moment ago? "I didn't go to

Whiskey Mountain Lodge today," she said. "I went to lunch with someone else. A man."

Ryder blinked, confusion entering his expression now. "You're seeing someone else? Already?"

"My sons set it up," she said. "We've been out once or twice."

"Which is it?" Ryder demanded. "Once? Or twice? Is this—do you like him?"

Finn at least made her stomach tighten and her pulse accelerate. She hadn't seen him in a cowboy hat yet, and she wondered if that would kill the chemistry between them.

Only if you let it, drifted through her mind, and she couldn't get rid of the thought though she tried.

Amanda also didn't quite know how to answer Ryder. She'd been comfortable with Finn, at least once they'd started talking. There were new things in their relationship, sure, and that created a bit of awkwardness.

But looking at Ryder, all she could feel was annoyance and pity. "I'm sorry," she said, turning to take the soup inside. She could get the tortilla strips and leftover sour cream later.

"Amanda," Ryder said. "You're sure about this other guy?"

She rounded on him, wishing she didn't feel a shower of sparks rushing through her bloodstream when she pictured Finn in her mind. "Yes, Ryder," she said, deciding on the spot. "We've been out twice now, and I like the *man*."

He wasn't a guy, that much had been obvious from the first moment Amanda had laid eyes on Finn.

Ryder looked like he'd say something else, then he lifted his hands in the air and fell back a step. "All right. Okay. Good luck with him." He turned and strode away, sending relief through Amanda's muscles.

She hit the button to close the garage door, hurried inside the house, and closed the door behind her, clicking the lock into place before heading into the kitchen and setting down the heavy soup pot.

Her house was too big for her. She knew that. She paid someone to keep the grounds looking nice. To come in once a week and keep everything dust-free and polished and smelling good.

She did her own laundry, all the dishes, and she enjoyed cooking. Well, she did when she had the opportunity to share her food with someone else. "Like today," she said, flipping on a couple of lights and getting to work putting the soup in plastic containers.

Yes, she'd really liked today, and while she had some reservations about Finn, she had just used him to get rid of another man. And she hadn't lied. She did like Finn.

"Too much already," she muttered to herself. Beans rang the bell on the sliding glass door behind the kitchen table, and Amanda moved to let her out. Finn hadn't called or texted in the hour since she'd left his house, and that was fine. She didn't need him smothering her.

Would it be smothering if she texted him right now?

Because she'd pretty much decided she wanted to see

him again, and they didn't have anything scheduled or set up.

She put the soup away, let Beans back in, and went through her nighttime skin care routine before she even allowed herself to pick up her phone again.

What's your schedule like this week?

She stared at the message, wondering what Finn would think of it. She wasn't even sure what she thought of it.

She sent it anyway, hoping she wasn't coming on too strong, but fearing she was. After all, she'd invited herself out to his place for lunch too.

Cursing herself, she plugged in her phone, silenced it, and got in bed. No, she wasn't sixteen, but she sure did feel inexperienced when it came to dating a man like Finn Barber.

CHAPTER 6

Finn woke to more flashing lights on his phone, a special kind of exhaustion following him as he went into the kitchen to start the coffee he couldn't live without. All three dogs came with him, and he found the clicking of their claws on the wood floor comforting.

He deliberately kept his phone face-down on the counter as he cracked several eggs into a pan. "There will be plenty for all of us, guys," he told the canines as he stepped to open the door so they could go outside.

They all seemed to smile at him as he went by, and he couldn't help chuckling as their tails whipped by him. He left the door open, because the morning air felt cool and fresh, and went back to making breakfast.

His mind revolved around the multiple things he had to accomplish that day, and he decided to leave his phone right where it was. Surely any messages he got could be answered later.

Just as the eggs finished, Chocolate came back inside as if he knew his breakfast was ready. Finn divided up the eggs across four plates and put three of them on the floor. "Leave it," he said to Chocolate, just as Vanilla and Licorice came tumbling back into the house.

"Leave it," he commanded again.

All three pups stopped moving, their eyes trained on him. If he let Vanilla go first, he'd gobble up his plate of eggs and then try to shove Licorice out of the way to get his too. Chocolate, the oldest Lab, would go first, and Finn stepped in front of Vanilla and said, "Okay, Choc."

He practically dove forward, and Finn said, "Licorice." Vanilla twitched, but Finn held out his hand toward the dog, his palm practically in his face. The plates scraped the floor as the other two dogs ate, and a whine started in Vanilla's throat.

"All right," he said to him, and the yellow Lab nearly knocked Finn down in his haste to get to his eggs.

Finn shook his head, a smile on his face, as he returned to the bar for his own breakfast. The call of that blue light tugged at him until he reached for his phone, his eggs cold already anyway.

Only one message, and from the best person. Amanda had asked him what his schedule was for the week, and he simply looked at the words. Why didn't he know how to answer her?

"Maybe because you don't really have a schedule," he

said to the empty house. He had work to do, and he did it, moving from task to task based on the time of day, especially in the winter.

For example, he was already a little late getting outside for the morning weeding and animal feeding, and if he didn't hurry up, he'd be battling the heat and the sun to get those chores done.

He left his eggs on the counter and headed for the mudroom where he kept his work boots and his cowboy hat. Properly attired, he did end up shoving his phone in his back pocket without replying to Amanda's text. After all, if he had an accident out on the farm, he'd need a way to call for help.

At that moment, he remembered he'd been inspired to call his daughter. Once outside with all the dogs, he closed the sliding door behind him to keep the air conditioning inside where it belonged.

He took out his phone and called Joann, hoping his daughter still didn't go to work until noon.

"Hey, Daddy," she said, though she'd turned thirty in the spring.

"Joann," he said with a smile. "How are things at the restaurant?"

"Oh." She exhaled heavily. "Same as always, I suppose. Teenagers coming and going all the time. Slow drive-through times. Same old stuff." She laughed, and Finn did too, because he knew that while Joann's restaurant brought her a lot of stress, there was nothing she'd rather be doing.

"Any new boyfriends?" he asked.

She groaned. "No, Dad. Not you too. Mom's been actually trying to set me up with people." The disgust in her voice wasn't hard to hear.

Finn chuckled. "We both just want you to be happy," he said.

"I know," she said. "But I'll say the same thing to you that I said to her. What makes you think a boyfriend would make me happy? Maybe I'm doing just fine on my own."

"Of course you are," he said, surprised at the fire in his daughter. "I was just making conversation."

"I know." She sighed. "Besides, it's not like you can talk. When's the last time you went out with someone?"

Finn very nearly tripped over his own feet as he walked toward the stables. "Actually...."

"Dad," Joann practically shrieked. "This is why you called, isn't it? Who is she?"

Finn chuckled, heat rising through him despite the cool air. "I wanted to talk to you, because...well, I don't really know why."

"How did you meet her?"

"Blind date," he said.

"Oh, come on," Joann said. "That's not true."

"It is," Finn said, laughing. "Honest, honey. A friend of mine set me up with his mother. Now, I didn't know it was his mother...." He continued the story, including as much detail as he felt appropriate, and then said, "And I'm not quite sure. I mean, she feels like my complete opposite. She's a little overbearing, always texting and stuff."

"Dad, that's what people do," she said. "She's dated other men in the past five years. She knows how it's done."

"I don't think she likes cowboys." He reached up and touched his hat as if it were a brand.

"You don't know that," Joann said. "You're speculating. And what do you always tell me about speculation?"

"That it's probably not true," he said in a deadpan.

"Right," she said. "So why not? I can tell you like her, even if you've only known her for a day. What's the big deal? You know people meet online and fall in love without even seeing each other in person, right?"

Finn did not know that, and he didn't need to know that. "I'm just worried, I guess," he said. "Like maybe this isn't the right thing to do."

"Why wouldn't it be? Dad, Mom's happy. We're all happy. You might as well be happy too."

"Yeah," he said, but it wasn't about happiness. He knew that. Joann moved the conversation to her sister, and Finn said he'd call Kim too, and then hung up.

He got the horses out of the stables and into the pastures for the day. He fed the chickens. Got all the animals fresh water. He cleaned out stalls when the sun was overhead, and returned to the cool house for lunch.

As he wished he had some of that tortilla soup from yesterday, he realized his real problem. He didn't feel worthy of a second chance at love and marriage. After all, he'd messed up so spectacularly the first time, and he was perfectly happy with his horses, chickens, and dogs.

Wasn't he?

As he spread mayo on bread and added ham and cheese, a niggling feeling inside told him that no, he wasn't "perfectly happy." Amanda had filled a hole he hadn't even known existed in his life. Or rather, one he knew was there, but thought couldn't be filled.

He took a bite of his sandwich and pulled out his phone.

I work for myself, he typed out. *My schedule can be rearranged.* He sent the message, and then quickly started tapping again.

How about lunch tomorrow? I'll come pick you up. Say twelve-thirty?

That would get him out of the heat in the hottest part of the day, and he'd get to see Amanda again. He felt powerful for asking her this time instead of letting himself be set up or accepting her suggestion of bringing him lunch.

Sure, she responded, followed with her address and the words *See you then.*

Excitement popped through Finn, and he whistled to himself as he finished lunch and went to work on the yard.

THE FOLLOWING DAY, his palms felt slick as he pulled into the driveway of the appointed address. "Wow," he said, gazing at the long driveway with the immaculate yard on both sides. This woman definitely had money, because there was no way she did all this yardwork herself.

The house itself spanned two stories and looked like it could easily sleep two dozen people. He knew who Amanda Whittaker was, of course. Her husband had owned the largest energy company in the state, and her son had invented the robotics that had taken them out of the league of anyone else drilling for natural gas in Wyoming.

She was a billionaire, same as Finn, and he had strange thoughts of finally meeting someone who could possibly like him for simply who he was. Not which family he came from. Not how many champion horses he'd bred and trained. Not how many zeroes he had in his bank account.

The doorbell echoed throughout the countryside, and Amanda herself opened the door a few seconds later. "Hey," she said, scanning him from head to toe. Her eyes came back to his face—and the cowboy hat he wore. "I'm not sure I know you...what can I do for you, cowboy?"

Her eyes glittered pure flirtation at him, and Finn chuckled.

"I guess I'm your cowboy blind date," he said, reaching for her hand. "Does the hat bother you?" He watched her as sparks joined his bloodstream from the softness of her skin, the easy way she let him touch her.

"No," she said, her voice a little high and a little false.

"You can be honest," he said.

She sighed and stepped back into the house for a

moment to grab her purse. "All right. I did tell my sons I didn't want a cowboy blind date."

"Ah." He nodded, took her hand again after she'd exited the house, and started slowly for the steps. "Well, I wasn't a cowboy at the restaurant."

"No," she said slowly. "But you are a cowboy."

"That I am, ma'am." He paused at the top of the stairs. "If that's going to be a problem for you, maybe we should forgo lunch." His entire being wailed at the thought, and he couldn't believe that just yesterday morning he was contemplating not perpetuating a relationship with Amanda at all.

She looked at him. Reached up and touched the brim of his hat. Smiled. "I don't think it's going to be that big of a problem."

"Really?" He didn't mean to sound so surprised.

"Maybe we should just play it by ear," she said, tugging on his hand gently to get him to come down the steps with her. He did, thinking he'd probably follow her wherever she wanted to go.

Then he reminded himself he was in charge of today's date. That he wanted to be the one asking her out and picking her up and surprising her. His daughter's words rang in her ears. *She's dated a lot in the past five years. She knows how it's done.*

Finn did not. Had not. But he didn't just want to be Amanda's lap dog. "So there's this great place a few miles from here. They make everything in a Dutch oven. Have you been there?"

"No," she said. "In Coral Canyon?"

"No, it's out on the road between here and Etna."

"Sounds intriguing." She smiled at him, and he stepped in front of her to open the passenger door on his truck. Amanda wore a pair of jeans and a blouse with wildflowers on it, and she smelled like heaven. Finn couldn't help leaning in and taking a deep breath as he put his hand on the small of her back and helped her into the truck.

He had several nice vehicles, and he was secretly glad for them as he walked around the front of the truck and got behind the wheel. He wanted to impress this woman, and he wasn't sure if he should be glad he could or worried he wasn't going to be himself.

"Tell me about growing up in Kentucky," she said as he turned around to leave her property. He dang near drove into a pine tree he jerked the wheel so hard.

Amanda just smiled at him. "Ah, I see I struck a nerve."

Try a thousand nerves, he thought, staring at her, completely unsure of how to begin.

CHAPTER 7

Amanda wanted to give Finn a way out. Ask him another question. But at the same time, her curiosity over why his childhood was so difficult to talk about intrigued her. So she simply waited.

He drove to the end of the lane and turned onto the street. "I grew up the oldest of two brothers," he said. "The boarding stables and racehorse business should've been mine."

"You have boarding stables and a racehorse business," she said. "Here."

"Exactly," he said. "Here. Not there. My father was...." He cut her a look out of the corner of his eye. "A drunk. A mean one. Taught me everything I needed to know to run the family business, sure. Taught me how to drown my troubles and disappointments in a bottle too."

Amanda recoiled from the words. "Oh, I'm sorry, Finn. I didn't know."

"I'm fifty-five-years-old," he said. "I have a past. It's fine. I don't mind telling you about it."

"No?" Because he seemed to mind.

"It's hard to talk about sometimes," he said, keeping one hand loosely on the wheel while the other one rested on the windowsill beside him. He seemed to be the perfectly calm, collected man she wanted.

Oops, not man. *Cowboy.*

And she hated to admit it, but he was extremely sexy in that cowboy hat. The boots. The jeans. The orange and white plaid shirt. All of it had her heart racing in a way it hadn't in years.

"Anyway," he said with a big sigh. "Once I got sober, I decided I didn't want the bourbon-drowned life my father had. I didn't want the unhappy marriage. I didn't want the bitter sons." He cast her a look she couldn't quite decipher before he looked back to the road. "The only thing I wanted was the horses. So I moved here, and I made it happen. Well, not Dog Valley immediately. I had a little operation outside of Jackson Hole for about fifteen years. Met my wife there. Started a family. It wasn't until that all broke up that I came to Dog Valley."

Amanda nodded, her head swimming with so much information. Finn had gone to church yesterday. He hadn't had anything to drink at the restaurant on Saturday night, and she hadn't seen alcohol in his house.

"Do you still drink?" she asked.

"Not even a drop, ma'am," he said. "You?"

"No, sir," she said. "My poison is along the lines of

potato chips and chocolate. Not together." She laughed. "Or maybe together. I've never really tried them together."

He smiled, and the light of it filled the whole cab. "I like black coffee and banana bread to dip in it," he said. "Can't get a better meal than that."

"Sounds like a snack," she said playfully.

"Maybe it is," he agreed.

Amanda reveled in the happiness pulling through her. He'd just told her something difficult, and she knew so much more about him now. "When did you move to Wyoming?" she asked.

"Oh, let's see," he said. "I was twenty-one, so thirty-four years ago."

"I moved from Dallas when I was eighteen," she said.

"Really? Dallas? I don't hear any Texas in you." He grinned at her, and she couldn't help laughing lightly.

"My parents were not happy," she said. "I was barely an adult, and I left behind my family, my college scholarship. All of it."

"Your husband must've been something special," Finn said his voice getting a little quieter.

Amanda took a moment to answer. "He was a unique man, yes," she said. "I loved him, but he wasn't without his flaws."

"None of us are," Finn said, and Amanda smiled.

"Of course not." She folded her hands in her lap, a keen sense of missing moving through her. Yes, she'd loved Ronald and the beautiful, comfortable life he provided for her. "The truth is, Finn, I was just as lonely before Ron died as I am now."

That brought his attention to her, and Amanda tried to smile again. It felt a little unsure on her face, and she tucked her hair behind her ear. "He worked a lot. More than a lot. I...found other ways to fill my time, and losing him was hard. But not in the ways you might imagine."

Foolishness raced through her. What had she just said? That she loved her husband but didn't miss him? Why did she feel like she missed him, then?

She shook her head. "I don't know what I'm saying."

"I think you do," Finn said quietly, making another turn. "And I work a lot, too, Amanda. Comes with taking care of animals."

She looked at him and found the concern in his eyes, the clear question of his workload being a deal-breaker for her. "You're taking me to lunch in the middle of the day. Actual lunchtime. My husband never did that."

"Okay," Finn said, accelerating now that they were out of town. He aimed the truck north, and Amanda turned to watch the scenery go by. She couldn't believe her choice of conversation topics, and she once again felt way out of her league when it came to Finn. Dating other men hadn't been this...tumultuous, and she wondered what the difference was.

"Here we are," he said a few minutes later, easing the truck off the road and into a dirt parking lot beside a building.

"I didn't know someone had bought this place," she

said, peering through the windshield at a clearly hand-painted sign that said The Open Fire. A picture of three Dutch ovens sat in flames, and she smiled at the simplicity of the place. "There are several cars here."

"It's good," Finn said. "If you like this kind of food."

She felt the weight of his eyes on the side of her face, and she turned toward him. "I'm sure I will." She reached for the door handle and slid to the ground, glad she hadn't worn a skirt for lunch. She'd wanted to, but in the end, it had felt too formal. Like she was trying too hard.

Finn met her at the front of the truck, taking her hand and lifting it to his lips. "When can I see you again?" he asked, his voice low and filled with emotion.

"You're seeing me now," she said, nudging him with her shoulder in a flirty way.

"I know." He ducked his head and smiled. "I just want to have something else on the calendar to look forward to." He met her eyes, and she saw an earnestness there she really liked. "I might be a little lonely too, and you make it less so."

She searched his face, sure she hadn't heard him right. Most men weren't as forward with their feelings as Finn had just been, even the older ones she'd dated.

"Friday night?" he asked, leaning forward like he'd kiss her cheek. He didn't, but pressed his against hers, so his next, whispered words sent shivers down her spine. "The old city hall in Turnersville has dinner and dancing every Friday night."

"Is that right?" she asked, thinking of the last time a

man had asked her to dance. It had been Ron, in Dallas, the night she'd fallen in love with him. Forty-four years ago.

"Mm hmm," Finn hummed in her ear. "The food's terrible, but the dancing is pretty fun."

"Do you know how to dance, cowboy?" she asked, feeling eighteen again, full of life and light and like her future held endless possibilities.

"I'm not half-bad." He pulled away, putting a respectable distance between them. "It's forty minutes to Turnersville from Coral Canyon. Dinner is at six. I could pick you up."

"I'd like that," she said with a smile, her stomach swooping at the next date with this gorgeous man. She reached up and re-centered his hat on his head and added, "Now, come on. I'm starving, and you promised me lunch in the middle of the day."

He tipped his head back and laughed, and Amanda decided it was the best sound in the world.

❦

"IS THAT WHAT HE SAID?" Amanda asked later that evening, the lunch with Finn still swirling through her head.

"That's what he said," Lois Jensen said, pulling down the husks on another ear of corn. "Can you believe it?"

"I honestly don't know," Amanda said to her best friend and once-next-door neighbor. She ripped out all the silk on the ear of corn in her hand. "It just doesn't seem like a tractor should cost that much."

"Well, it's not like it used to be." Lois shook her head, her trim pixie cut barely moving. Amanda had wanted to cut her hair like her friend's for a while now, but she hadn't been quite brave enough.

"But Walt's doing okay in Oklahoma City?" she asked.

"Seems to be," Lois said, reaching for another ear of corn. "I keep telling him he'll have to give up the farming conferences soon, but he doesn't believe me." She shook her head and clucked her tongue. "That man. He's going to be the death of me." She laughed, and Amanda did too. Walt and Lois had lived down the street from Amanda and Ron while they raised their kids, and they'd been through thick and thin together. Sicknesses, traveling husbands, kids getting in car accidents, going off to college, getting married, all of it.

Amanda didn't know what she would've done without Lois when Ron had died. She sat up straighter and cleared her throat. "I'm seeing someone new."

"Oh, boy," Lois said, looking up from her work. She paused, her eyes catching on Amanda's. "Oh, this seems different than Ryder."

"He is different than Ryder," Amanda said. "And Jason." She tried not to sigh after his name, but she failed.

"Who is he?"

"Finn Barber," she said, reminding herself that she and Jason were not the right match. "He lives out in Dog Valley."

"Tell me you won't move to Dog Valley," Lois said. "Amanda, please."

"Don't sound so horrified," she said, shaking her head. "I went out there on Sunday, and it wasn't so bad."

"You're kidding."

"They've really spruced the place up in the last twenty years, Lois." Amanda gave her friend a look. "You'd know that if you ever left Coral Canyon."

"Why do I need to leave?" Lois puffed out her chest. "Everything I need is right here."

"You know this corn didn't come from Coral Canyon, right?"

"It was on the red flatbed in the parking lot at Jenner's." Lois kept her eyes on her ear of corn.

"It's too early for corn in Wyoming." Amanda shook her head, knowing Lois knew this. Heck, she had a whole garden full of corn that was at least two months away from being ripe.

"So you went to Dog Valley already. Weren't you just dating Ryder last week?"

"A couple weeks ago," she said. "Graham and Beau set me up with Finn. We've been out a few times is all."

"And you're telling me already."

"Well, I won't see you again until you need help with the raspberry jam." Amanda threw her friend a knowing look.

"Not true," Lois said. "You're doing that baby quilt tying event at your place next month. I'd have come for that."

"Oh, of course," Amanda said with some heavy sarcasm. She and Lois used to go to lunch as young mothers, and she still enjoyed seeing her friend. But they didn't have as many stressors as they'd had when they were younger, and they mostly spent time together now when one of them needed help with a big project.

"How's Kevin doing with the gardening?" she asked.

"Great," Lois said. "He's busy, he said."

Amanda glanced at her friend, sensing they'd moved onto chatting about their kids. As Lois launched into how well her son's landscaping business was doing, her suspicions were confirmed.

Hey, at least she hadn't had to answer any questions about her and Finn, the fact that he owned a huge farm and probably owned a dozen cowboy hats, or her trip to Dog Valley.

But secretly, she couldn't wait for Friday night when she'd get to see him again.

CHAPTER 8

Finn slammed on the brakes at the same time he swerved to the side of the road. "What in the world is she doing?" he muttered to himself. He put the truck in reverse and backed up to the house he'd just passed.

Sure enough, old Nancy Goodman was trying to heave a box out of the back of the tiny sedan she shared with her sister.

"Nancy," he called as soon as he got his window down. "Let me help you with that." He was no spring chicken himself, but the Goodman sisters had several years on him, and Nancy had been in for back surgery just last fall. No way she should be lifting anything more than her purse.

He hurried to park the truck and get out, jogging over to the trunk of the car. "How are you?" he asked, lifting the fifty-pound box of frozen chicken tenders.

"Good, good," she said. "Big sale on chicken right now."

"I can see that." He grinned at her and started for the front door. "Where's Kelly?"

"Oh, she went to see our cousin in town," she said, fitting her key in the lock. Finn literally never locked his house, and he almost starting laughing. He did, however, lock down his stables, so he supposed he couldn't fault Nancy for keeping things secure at home.

Inside, the ratty furniture and nicked dining room table testified otherwise. They'd probably be better off if someone broke in and stole these things. But then Nancy would never sleep in the house again. Over the years of living down the road from them, he'd learned that Kelly was the stable one. The younger sister who took care of the house, the yard, and the bills.

Nancy suffered from a variety of health problems, both mental and physical, and Finn had come by to take care of their yard more than once in the last twenty years.

"Where do you want this?" he asked, seeing the kitchen counter was full of things. Dishes, towels, notebooks.

"Just set it there," she said, going straight for the recliner and collapsing into it. Her breath wheezed through the house, and Finn had the strangest urge to open all the blinds and all the windows. Let in some fresh air and some light to breathe life into this place.

"I'll get the rest," he said cheerfully, retracing his steps to the car to get the rest of the groceries. As he unpacked them and started opening cupboards to find where things went, he asked, "How did Kelly get to town if you have the car?"

"Selena came and picked her up," Nancy said, and Finn detected some jealousy there. He didn't know what to do about it, as he didn't spend a lot of time with the sisters. He mostly just watched out for them and helped when and where he could.

"Your birthday is coming up, isn't it?" he asked, opening the freezer to see if there was room for the chicken inside. Not even a little bit. Frustration pulled through him, as he was already running a bit late to get home, shower, and get back to Coral Canyon in time to pick up Amanda for their dinner and dancing date that night.

"Yes," Nancy said. "It's in a few weeks."

"I'm sure Kelly will make you a nice cake," he said. "Nancy, do you have a chest freezer? In the garage maybe?" He started toward the door that must lead to the garage.

"No," she barked. "And you can't go out there." She got to her feet awkwardly, but quickly, and approached him. "I'll take care of the chicken. Thanks so much, Finn." She practically shoved him out onto the porch, and he was surprised enough to just go.

She closed the door with a smile that looked half genuine and half panicked, and Finn stood there wondering what had just happened.

His mind whirred, going down all kinds of strange and

delusional paths. Surely he'd have noticed a smell if they had a body or something out there.... Right?

"Not if it's in the freezer," he muttered, sure these two nice little old ladies didn't have any bodies in their garage. He couldn't help that his mind had gone there, and he went down the steps and around the side of the house.

The garage had windows on this side, and he cupped his hands to peer through the dirty glass. It took him several long moments to realize what he was looking at.

"Trash," he said. "Even if there was a body in there, they'd never find it." So they were hoarders. Or at least one of them was, though he hadn't noticed it being too terrible inside the house. Sure, it had a smell, and yes, there were things piled everywhere. But nothing like he'd seen on those reality TV shows.

He got in the truck, satisfied his nearest neighbors weren't going to pose any danger to him, and went home. The dogs jumped down from the back of the truck, Licorice barking as the three of them rounded the front corner of the house on their way to the bigger backyard.

He cracked the door off the deck so they could get in when they wanted to, and he jumped in the shower.

And hour later, he pulled up to Amanda's house to find her sitting in one of the rocking chairs on the front porch. As he climbed the steps, he admired the pretty white dress she wore, with colorful flowers embroidered along the hem and down the sleeves.

"Don't you look nice?" he asked, sitting in the chair on the other side of the small table.

"Thank you," she said, indicating the second glass of lemonade sitting there. "It's not black coffee, but it's much too hot for that anyway."

He lifted the glass to his lips. "Did you make this?" he asked, the sourness making his taste buds cramp before he'd even taken a sip.

"I sure did."

He drank then, pure pleasure rolling through him at the tangy yet sweet liquid. "It's delicious," he said.

"Are you ready for dancing?" she asked, standing up.

He let her take his hand though he didn't need her help getting up. He kept her fingers in his and pulled her close to him. "You're stunning," he whispered, feeling sparks come alive in every part of his body. "I feel like the luckiest man in the world."

Amanda giggled, grabbed onto his shoulders, and they swayed right there on her porch. "Don't get too excited yet, cowboy," she said. "You haven't seen me dance, and I'm pretty sure I have two left feet."

Finn didn't even care. He just wanted to be with Amanda, and that concept alone was foreign enough to have him simply sweeping his lips along her cheekbone and saying, "All right. Let's go."

The food at the dinner wasn't good, as Finn had predicted it wouldn't be. He leaned toward Amanda and whispered, "We'll get something good on the way home, okay?"

She'd put her fork down at that moment, and once the table and chairs had been cleared, it was time for dancing.

"May I?" he asked, bowing slightly and offering her his hand.

She giggled again, and while she was a mature woman, the sound elicited something inside him Finn thought he'd never feel again.

Desire.

He wanted to kiss her right then and there on the dancefloor, but he didn't. He knew it was too early, and he certainly didn't want their first kiss to be in front of anyone else.

"My sons are hosting a Cupcake Wars event at the lodge in a couple of weeks," Amanda said, swaying easily with him. "Everyone needs a partner to participate, and I thought maybe you'd like to be mine."

Warmth filled Finn, and he grinned down at her. "What does that entail?"

"You have to try to beat my cupcakes," she said, a sly smile on those full lips. "So you bake your cupcakes, fill them, frost them, decorate them. Then everyone judges and a winner is declared."

Finn spun her away from him and snapped her right back into his arms. "And what gave you the idea that I know how to bake?" He wasn't even sure why cupcakes needed to be filled.

She clung to his shoulders in such a way that Finn would've probably declared he could build a submarine if she said she'd spend time with him while he did it. She tipped her head back as she laughed, and Finn couldn't help staring at her throat.

Her very kissable throat.

Reining in his fantasies, he managed to smile at her when she looked at him. "So we wouldn't really be partners. We'd be competing against each other."

"I can see if they're doing partners this time," she said. "They started doing it every so often about a year ago. Jason and I—" She went mute as if someone had pressed a button behind her ear that made her vocal chords turn off.

Finn watched the panic parade across her face. He leaned down as the song slowed. With her fully in his arms, he said, "Amanda, I know you dated before me."

She said nothing but pressed in closer to him.

"Was Jason your last boyfriend?" he asked.

"No," she whispered. "Ryder was, but we only went out for a couple of weeks. Jason and I...we were together for just over two and a half years."

"Years?" Finn couldn't help the incredulity from his voice. He pulled back a little and looked at her. "Really? That long?" Why would anyone date Amanda for that long and not make her his? Put a diamond on that finger? Heck, Finn was already thinking about it, and he'd met her a week ago.

"We had a very complicated relationship," she said, swallowing afterward. "Anyway, he and I competed as a team once in the family shenanigans of cupcake baking."

"Did you win?" he asked, somehow needing to know. As if it mattered. He didn't even know who Jason was, but it was clear by the look on Amanda's face that he'd been important to her.

A thin veil of jealousy moved through Finn, and he didn't even know why. Amanda wasn't seeing Jason anymore.

"No," she said. "We didn't win. Celia is very good in the kitchen."

"Oh, right." He smiled, knowing exactly who Celia was. Graham had hired her at the lodge to cook, and she'd been there for almost as long as Graham had been back in town.

"I'll find out if it's partners or one-on-one, okay?" she asked.

"Sure," he said.

"I'd love for you to meet everyone," she said. "Is that too fast?"

Finn felt like lightning had struck him, the powerful waves of electricity moving through his muscles and frying them. He hadn't even thought of meeting her sons, their wives, her friends, everyone at the lodge.

Of course, he already knew Graham and Beau. Meeting a few others wouldn't be that hard.

"Sure," he said again, wishing he could think of more to say. Thankfully, the band picked up the tempo, and she squealed as he spun her again.

By the time the night ended, Finn's heart had really gotten a workout—and not only from the dancing.

He drove Amanda back to her private estate set back off the road and walked her to the front door.

"That was the most fun I've had in ages," she said, smiling up at him.

"Me too," he said honestly. He wanted to kiss her, but she put her hand on the doorknob and went inside.

"Night, cowboy," she said, her voice sultry and full of flirt.

"Night, ma'am," he said, tipping his hat to her and backing up.

She brought the door closed, and Finn sighed a happy little sound that held the promise of a kiss another day.

He couldn't wait, and he wondered how long she'd make him do so. Or if she even wanted to kiss him at all.

With new worries in his mind, he drove back to Dog Valley and the three things that he never doubted: his dogs.

CHAPTER 9

A manda spent most of Saturday thinking about Finn, but she did not want to contact him first. She really liked the warm fuzzies she got when he asked her to dinner, to dance, or anything else.

She worked in her vegetable garden in the morning, and she bought all the ingredients for fresh salsa and spent the afternoon with tomatoes and cilantro. Finn hadn't texted by evening, and she said yes when Andrew and Becca asked her to babysit Chrissy.

They pulled up to her house right on time, and Chrissy laughed as she waddled toward Amanda when they set her down just inside the door.

"Hey, baby," she drawled, a smile on her face. "Come see Grandma. That's right. Good girl. Come on."

Beans tried to knock the two-year-old down, but Chrissy paused and patted the dog, who was the perfect height for her.

"Thanks, Mom," Andrew said, coming in after his daughter. "How are things going with Finn?"

Amanda scooped her granddaughter into her arms and giggled with her. She needed a few seconds to gather her thoughts on Finn. No, she hadn't kissed him last night, though he'd had the glint in his eye that said he was interested, and Amanda's own nerves testified of the same thing.

But she was older now, and she wasn't going to be ruled by her hormones, whims, or fancies.

"Going pretty good, actually," she said, looking at her son openly.

Andrew leaned down, his cowboy hat bumping her forehead as he tried to kiss her cheek. "I'm glad, Mom." He stayed close and said, "We're having another baby. Becca didn't want to tell anyone yet, but I'm super excited."

Joy burst through Amanda, and she grabbed onto her son and hugged him. "Congratulations, Andy. I won't say anything to anyone."

He squeezed her tight and stepped back, happiness streaming from him too. "You should come have lunch at the office this week," he said.

"Sure," Amanda said. "Name the day. I'm pretty open."

"Really? You're not spending every day with Finn?"

"Oh, get out of here. Your pregnant wife is waiting for you." Amanda swatted at him, but he easily dodged her playful gesture.

He laughed, backing up a few steps. "Love you, Ma."

"Love you too, son." She watched him walk out, happy for him and Becca. It had taken Andrew a long time to see there was more to life than Springside Energy, and she was glad he finally had. He and Becca both worked for the company, and without them, things would've fallen apart a long time ago.

"He's doing great, Ron," she whispered to the empty house, drawn back to reality by the babbling baby in her arms.

"Cream, cream, cream," Chrissy said, wiggling to get down.

"Yes," Amanda said. "Ice cream. Let's go get it, baby." She followed Chrissy at a snail's pace, nothing else to fill her time but this sweet little girl. "Chocolate?" she asked. "Strawberry?"

She opened the freezer and pulled out both containers, crouching down in front of her granddaughter. "Chocolate or strawberry?"

"Berry," Chrissy said, and Amanda put the chocolate back in the freezer.

"That's my favorite too, baby," she said. "Beans loves it too." She scooped up three bowls of ice cream and put Chrissy in the booster seat at her kitchen table. Beans got her tiny spoonful on the floor, and Amanda sat at the table too.

Babysitting Chrissy was easy, because she was a happy, chubby little girl who liked blocks as well as puzzles as well as coloring. Or Amanda could put a movie on, and Chrissy would be asleep in an hour.

Her phone snapped out her texting sound a few minutes later, and she glanced at it. Finn had finally texted.

Want to come out to the farm one day this week? I'll make you my favorite meatballs and gravy, with scalloped potatoes.

Amanda grinned at the invitation. *Finally,* ran through her mind, and she realized maybe she just needed to slow down when it came to him. Relief filled her that she hadn't kissed him last night, even if they'd both been thinking about it.

Amanda knew better than most that there was a huge difference between thinking about something and actually doing it.

Sounds like winter food, Amanda typed out. *But there's nothing I like more than meat and potatoes.*

He didn't answer right away, and she got up and put all the bowls in the sink. "Ready for coloring?" she asked Chrissy, who clapped her hands.

Amanda got out paper and crayons before Finn texted again. *Tell me what day works for you.*

She wanted to see Finn sooner rather than later, but she didn't want to seem overeager. *Tuesday?* she sent.

Tuesday it is. See you then.

Amanda felt like she could walk on water as she watched her granddaughter scribble on the paper in front of her. "Should we put on some music?" she asked, turning toward her Internet radio speaker and telling it to play nursery rhymes.

Chrissy looked up, her smile instant. "Humpy," she

said, laughing as the song for Humpty Dumpty started playing in the house. She babbled along happily to the music, getting some of the words in the right place.

Amanda smiled, content with her life in this moment. A beautiful granddaughter. A date on the horizon with a handsome man.

Not just a man, she thought. *A cowboy.*

And the thought was just fine inside her mind. In fact, it fit right inside her life.

THE NEXT DAY, she spent the morning in church beside Beau and Lily, one grandson on her lap and another sitting beside her on the bench. She barely heard the pastor, and she wouldn't have it any other way. She helped Ronnie with his shoelace while she held books for Charlie.

Afterward, she rode with Rose and Liam up to Whiskey Mountain Lodge, and it was a nice break from having to answer her son's questions about Finn. In fact, no one at the lodge asked her about him, and she had a great afternoon in the backyard of the lodge with Celia's famous potato salad and the scent of hot dogs and hamburgers filling the air.

Bailey rode horses while the littles played in the sandbox or got pushed in swings by their parents. Becca said nothing about her pregnancy, though Amanda noticed a glow about her that felt obvious.

Vi, however, stood up once Celia brought out the ice

cream. She looked around at everyone, and burst into tears.

"What's wrong?" Lily asked, jumping to her feet.

Vi pressed her lips together and shook her head, Rose going over to her as well, the three of them the famous Everett Sisters who'd given up their country music career to live in Coral Canyon, marry cowboys, and be mothers.

"Are you sick?" Rose asked, glancing at Todd. "Is it Todd again?"

Todd stood up, a smile on his face. He looked nervous, but he put his arm around Vi and said, "We're going to have a baby. Two, in fact."

Lily sucked in a breath at the same time Rose shrieked. She jumped up and down before covering her mouth with her hands. "Two babies?" she said through her fingers.

"The fertility treatments finally worked?" Lily asked, holding onto Vi's shoulders. "Really?"

"We heard the heartbeats on Friday," Vi said, her voice much too high and choked off. Her parents joined the Everett girls, and all the congratulations began. Amanda watched them, happy for Vi and Todd, though there was no blood relation between them.

When there was a break in the excitement, Amanda stood up and gave Vi a hug too. "Congratulations, dear." She moved to Todd. "And to you, Todd." She beamed at them, so much love up at this lodge.

She'd enjoyed so many events here with Jason, and she really wished she'd invited Finn to join her this afternoon.

Next week, she told herself, settling beside Graham and leaning closer. "Can I invite Finn to lunch next week?'

"I don't own the lodge," he said, not looking away from the horse Laney led with Bailey and Ronnie on it.

"Yes, you do," she said. "And you pay Celia."

"You've never asked me to invite your boyfriends before," he said, zeroing in on her now.

"I'm not asking if I can bring him," she said. "I know I can bring him."

"Then what are you asking?"

"I'm asking if it's too *early* to bring him to this kind of family gathering."

"I don't know, Mom. You do what you think is right."

She hated it when her sons threw her wisdom back in her face. For some reason, she couldn't decide what was right when it came to Finn.

Graham got up in the next moment, laughter spilling from his throat as his children did something cute with their horse. Amanda smiled at them. Smiled at Fran and Jack Everett. She belonged here, sure. But she felt removed at the same time.

She got up and went into the kitchen, almost hoping someone would call her back. They didn't. Celia stood there, setting the coffee cups into the maker. "Leaving already?" she asked, glancing up quickly.

"You know what?" Amanda asked. "I want to, but I don't have a ride." She turned back to the mudroom that led into the backyard, her plan to drive to Dog Valley and spend a couple of hours with Finn disappearing before her eyes. "I didn't think about that...."

"I'm headed back," she said. "Let me just go tell the kids that their coffee is on." Celia flashed her a smile and slipped out of the house. Amanda let her go, because she wanted to get back to her house and out to Dog Valley. And Celia probably didn't mind.

Five minutes later, she met Amanda in the parking lot in front of the lodge, another smile on her face. "Ready?"

"Yep." Amanda slid into the passenger seat of Celia's car and buckled her seat belt. The radio filled the silence, and it was a comfortable drive.

About halfway down the canyon, Celia said, "Can I ask you a question?"

"Of course," Amanda said, looking at the other woman. She was probably seven or eight years younger than Amanda. Not quite her generation, but close. She had some gray coming into her hair, especially in the front, and she'd had a short cut for as long as Amanda had known her.

"You've dated quite a bit since Ron died," Celia said, her fingers loosening and then tightening on the wheel. She swallowed. "How does one...I mean, if I wanted to start dating, how would I do that?" She shot Amanda a glance, and all of Amanda's unease at what Celia could ask fled.

She giggled and quickly covered her mouth with her hand. "I'm sorry," she said. "I didn't mean to laugh." She sobered and looked at Celia. "You're ready to start dating again?"

"Brandon died twenty years ago," Celia said. "I thought I was happy. I *am* happy. I just…."

"You're lonely," Amanda supplied. "The kids are great. You're great. You like your work. But there's something missing." She watched the pine trees. "Am I close?"

"Dead-on," Celia said.

"Let's go to lunch this week," Amanda said. "I'll tell you all my secrets."

And now her week was very, very full of lunch dates. Amanda smiled at the thought, glad she could help her friends and see Finn again.

CHAPTER 10

F inn answered Amanda's call when it came in, pulling off a glove to do it. "Hey," he said easily, glancing down the row in the henhouse. He hated the smell in here, and if was going to talk for any amount of time, he'd need to go outside.

He turned toward the door, deciding the eggs could wait a few minutes while he spoke on the phone.

"Where are you?" she asked.

"Out on the farm," he said.

"Oh, do you...would you mind if I joined you?"

He spun toward the house, but he could only see the corner of the deck from here. "You're in Dog Valley? Or on your way out?" Finn hoped she'd come, but he hadn't wanted to ask her. He'd opted for inviting her for lunch, hoping she'd find him downright irresistible if he cooked for her. Women liked that—at least he hoped they did.

"I'm standing on your porch, cowboy, and the wind is

worse here than in Coral Canyon." She conveyed plenty of flirtation in her voice, and Finn sure did like it. At the same time, he worried she'd left her family needlessly, and that he couldn't spare the entire evening to spend time with her.

"Walk around the side," he said. "Past the deck. There's a road that runs behind the house. Go left. You'll see the henhouse. I'll get the eggs, and meet you."

"All right," she said, to his surprise. "See you in a minute."

"Bye." He hung up, standing still for another moment, sure he hadn't heard right. Amanda was coming out on the farm. She didn't like farms.

"Or cowboys," he reminded himself. At the same time he pressed down his hat against that wind she'd spoken of, he remembered the sheer desire and delight in her eyes from Friday night. He'd lain awake for hours thinking about that look in her eye and wondering when he could ask her out again.

He'd made himself wait for twenty-four hours, and they had a lunch date on Tuesday.

And right now, he had eggs to gather. He ducked back into the henhouse, the stench twice as powerful as it had been five minutes ago. He started collecting the eggs, their shells an array of colors that brought peace to his soul. Light blue to white to brown, he loved the fresh eggs his hens provided.

When he finally burst out of the henhouse, he found

Amanda standing there in a pair of sneakers, jeans, and a red windbreaker.

She took his breath away, but some of that power belonged to the wind too. Dust kicked up into the air, obscuring the farm and making visibility only a few feet.

He squinted and said, "Holy cow," before reaching for Amanda's hand. "Let's go in the stables." He ducked his head against the dust and wind and headed for the building next door. As he reached for the door, the first rain drops fell.

Surprise mingled with his adrenaline as he burst into the stable. She laughed, and Finn's heartrate picked up with the sound of it.

"Whew," he said, taking off his hat and shaking the dirt off of it. He stepped over to the window, careful not to drop his eggs, and checked outside. "Looks like we're going to hunker down here for a minute."

The pounding sound of rain on the roof met his ears, and Amanda looked up to the ceiling. "It's so loud."

Energy filled the stables, and Finn turned toward his horses. He'd just brought them in before heading to the henhouse, and he hadn't seen the storm coming. Amanda apparently hadn't either.

"You want to meet the horses?" He set the eggs on a workbench and took her hand again. Feeling a bit reckless and a lot brave, he pulled her right against him, carefully wrapping both arms around her as he stared into her eyes. "It's good to see you."

She smiled and stroked both hands along the side of

his face, taking his hat off in what felt like an extremely intimate gesture. "Good to see you too."

"No family this afternoon?"

"I went to the lodge and had lunch with them," she said, her voice pitched slightly higher than normal.

"Wasn't enjoying yourself?" He cocked his head, feeling very exposed without his hat. Maybe Amanda just saw things in him that no one else had before.

She shrugged as much as she could in his arms. "I wanted to see you today."

He drew in a breath, and it was part perfume and sunshine, and part leather and horses. Stepping back, he put some distance between them. "I didn't think you liked farms or cowboys." He moved toward the first stall, where he kept Dark Beauty, a female racehorse who had great potential. In his heart of hearts, Finn knew he'd watch her win titles in the future.

"This is Dark Beauty," he said to Amanda when she didn't confirm or deny that she didn't like farms or cowboys. Frustration moved through him that she'd ignored him again, though the last time had been a week ago when he'd asked her about her family.

Maybe it was an oversight. At least that was what he told himself as the equine that could be a queen diva lifted her nose over the door of the stall. She huffed at him, but he didn't have any treats for her.

"This is Amanda," he said, cocking one hip into the door keeping the horse in her stall. "Amanda, Dark Beauty."

She looked at Finn like he'd lost his mind. Maybe he had. And he decided to be brave and reckless again. "Do you like farms and cowboys?" he asked. "Because if you don't, I'm just not sure we should keep seeing each other."

She blinked, her eyes widening. "I—"

Finn waited, because he was used to dealing with his horses, who had attitudes and a stubborn streak he had to keep intact and train out of them at the same time. They had to think they were more important than every other horse in the world so they'd run fast. And they had to love him and respect him at the same time.

Training a horse was tougher than it sounded, and dealing with jockeys was even tougher. The upcoming jockey training camp he did in August entered his mind, and he hadn't even started planning it yet.

Three months was a long time, but he should probably at least check and see if registrations were filling or not.

He wanted to sigh. Tell Amanda she should get on home. Get back to work so he could finish his chores and retire in front of the TV with a bowl of ice cream and a cup of coffee.

Finn waited another moment, and then another. Just as his frustration reached a boiling point, Amanda said, "I like *you*. And if you're a cowboy, then I guess I like cowboys."

He nodded and moved down to the next stall. He wasn't going to introduce her to any more horses, but a measure of comfort moved through him when she slipped her hand into his.

"Why don't you like cowboys?" he asked. "You got married young. Surely you didn't have a bad experience with one."

"I grew up in Texas," she said. "I've known dozens of cowboys, practically from the time I started school."

"Bad experience in kindergarten?" He chuckled. "Come on, Amanda. I'm not stupid."

"I didn't say you were stupid." She paused outside the next stall, this one for a horse named Always Boss. "He's beautiful."

"He's going to win some races, this one," Finn said fondly, drawing Amanda's attention. She gazed at him with all the adoration he'd always wanted from his wife. The desire he'd never quite seen in her eyes.

"I suppose I never wanted a cowboy because I didn't particularly like being a cowgirl."

He appreciated the honesty in her tone. "You don't have to be anything but what you already are."

A smile touched her face, radiating up into her eyes. "Thank you, Finn." She looped her arm in his and they walked down to the of the aisle and turned back.

"I think the rain has stopped," he said, listening for the patter of it on the roof and not hearing it. "We could make a run for it. I've got frozen cookie dough in the freezer, and you can make me some of that hot chocolate you were bragging about on Friday."

"I was not bragging," she said with a laugh.

Finn leaned over and kissed her cheek. "I know you weren't. Come on. Sometimes the rain only pauses for a second." As soon as he'd said it, he felt foolish. Of course, she'd already know that. She'd lived here for forty-five years.

She said nothing though, and Finn didn't press the issue of her not liking the farm. Her disinterest was obvious—almost as obvious as her interest in him. Was it possible for her to like—maybe even fall in love with—a cowboy and not like what he did for a living?

He supposed anything was possible, and he sent up a quick prayer as he gathered his basket full of eggs, cracked the door to check on the rain, and then hurried back to the house.

჻

THE NEXT EVENING, Finn had just taken the garlic bread out of the oven when the front door opened and his daughter called, "Dad?"

"In the kitchen," he said, hurrying to set the pan on top of the stove and toss the oven mitts to the counter beside that. He ducked around the corner and grinned at Joann and Kim, who'd driven out together from Jackson Hole.

"Smells amazing in here," Kim said, tossing her honey-blonde hair over her shoulder as she walked toward him, a smile on her pretty face.

"Hey, girls." He embraced them both, the three-way

hug making him feel like the best dad in the world, though he knew he wasn't. "How was the drive?"

"Joann nearly killed us at the crossroads," Kim said, tossing a look at her older sister.

"I did not. That trucker wasn't even looking." She handed Finn a package. "Mom said to give you this."

"Thanks." Finn looked at the small box, trying to figure out what his ex-wife would possibly have for him. Their mail hadn't been crossed in decades, and there was no reason he'd ever have something sent to her house. He didn't even know her address by heart.

"She said to open it right away." Joann lifted her eyebrows in such a way that Finn's fear boosted over his curiosity.

"What am I going to find?" he asked.

"I don't know," Joann said.

"If you don't open it, I will," Kim said from the kitchen. "I'm *starving,* and this food looks amazing."

It was just spaghetti and meatballs, but it was something Finn had been feeding his girls since they were little. He got nostalgic making it for them, though they were both grown now.

He lifted the flaps on the box, which had been tucked into one another. A candle sat inside, with the outline of the Teton Mountain Range on it.

"Ooh, a candle," Joann said, reaching inside the box. "I want one of these."

"They're made from organic beeswax," Kim said, as if Finn cared about such things. "And that one is scented with pine and nutmeg. It sounds weird, but it smells divine." She lifted the lid on the spaghetti and meatballs. "Can we eat now? We've been driving *forever.*"

Finn smiled at the dramatic whine of his youngest daughter. She'd always had a flair for exaggeration, and Finn had grown to love that about Kim.

"Sure," he said, taking the candle from Joann and setting it on the built-in desk in his kitchen he didn't actually use for anything but a gathering place for junk. Every once in a while, he'd clean it up. He opened the drawer and pulled out a lighter, got the wick burning, and turned to his daughters.

"Thank you so much for coming," he said, getting a little choked up.

"Of course, Daddy," Kim said. "Besides, Joann said you have a new girlfriend, and I want to hear all about her."

Finn just smiled and said, "Let's eat before I embarrass myself."

CHAPTER 11

Amanda worked through the next morning, paying bills, ordering groceries, and making flower-shaped sugar cookies for the widows in her church group. By the time she returned home from delivering them, the sun had heated the Wyoming landscape to almost unbearable temperatures, and it wasn't even June yet.

She had a few leftover cookies, and she tied ribbons around the cellophane and prepared them to take to her daughters-in-law. She stopped at Vi's first, though the woman wasn't technically related to her.

"Cookies," she said as she entered. Vi looked up from where she sat at the piano, a notebook open on her lap.

"Oh, Amanda," she said, jumping to her feet and practically throwing the notebook over her shoulder.

"I didn't mean to interrupt," she said, embarrassment

squirreling through her. The front door was open. It was just the screen."

"You didn't interrupt." Her eyes glittered at the cookie in Amanda's hand. "You're the best."

"I'm not Celia," Amanda said as she laughed and hugged Vi. "How are you feeling?"

"Great," she said. "Just fine."

"Where's Todd?" Neither of them had real jobs, as they both had money coming out their ears.

"He went to get lunch," she said. "We were just...." She looked at the piano and back to Amanda. "Can you keep a secret?"

"Nope," Amanda said. "I'm pretty terrible at it, actually." She laughed, glad when Vi joined in. All at once, she remembered she did have a secret, and she hadn't told anyone. "I take that back. I'm keeping a secret for someone right now, so I probably can do it."

Vi took a bite of her flower, taking off one petal. She chewed, looking thoughtful. After she swallowed, she said, "Todd and I are working on some new songs."

"Oh, wow," Amanda said. "That's great."

"For the babies," she said. "Todd's a great guitar player, and we want them to know how much we love them." Tears appeared in her eyes, and Amanda wanted to hug her tight, tight, tight.

"Oh, baby," she said. "They know you love them already."

Vi nodded, wiped her tears, and took another bite of her cookie. Amanda said she couldn't stay long, as she had other cookies to deliver, and she hugged Vi one last time before she left.

She remembered what a magical time it had been to be pregnant, and she thought about her life as a young mother as she drove to Rose's house. Rose wanted to be a mother more than anything, but Amanda hadn't heard any announcements yet.

No one was home, and she didn't dare leave the cookie to bake in the hot sun. So she took it with her and stopped by Becca's, only to find she wasn't home either. When Amanda texted her, she said she and Chrissy had gone to swimming lessons and would be back soon.

Deciding not to stay, Amanda left her cookie on the kitchen counter and went home. She stood in the foyer of the huge house she'd once shared with her husband. She loved this house. She'd designed this house with an architect, and it had everything exactly how she wanted it. Yes, the yard was too big. The pantry not big enough. So maybe not everything was exactly how she wanted it.

She doubted anything ever could be. Her marriage hadn't been perfect, but they'd made it work. She hadn't been a perfect mother, but somehow her sons had survived.

Standing in the silent house, she realized that maybe the reason none of her relationships had worked out over the past several years was because of her.

After all, she'd almost pushed Finn away because of a couple of accessories he wore. "It's more than that," she said to the vase of flowers on the front table.

Finn's entire way of life didn't appeal to Amanda. She didn't want to be tied to a farm, because animals needed constant care. If they went out of town, someone had to be there to take care of the chickens and horses and goats.

Not that Finn had goats. At least Amanda didn't think he did.

"And you don't travel," she said to herself. She had plenty of money, and she didn't particularly care to go anywhere. She wanted to be with her grandkids, her sons, their wives. And yet...she'd left the lodge yesterday.

Finn really had turned her entire world upside down, and she didn't even know which way to go anymore.

Her phone buzzed, and she retrieved it from her purse pocket. Finn had texted, as if he knew she'd been thinking about him. *Are you allergic to anything?*

She smiled at the simplicity of the message. He was probably nervous to cook for her, and she quickly sent back *Nope. And I like everything.*

That wasn't entirely true. She could do without cooked carrots or artichokes, but he'd said he was making meatballs and gravy with scalloped potatoes. Surely he couldn't put carrots in either of those.

"We'll find out tomorrow," she said, finally moving into the kitchen to discover she'd left a big, floury mess from the sugar cookies.

WHEN SHE PULLED up to Finn's the next day, she

found him getting his mail from the box at the end of his driveway. She stopped and rolled down her window. "Need a ride, partner?" She laughed, and Finn grinned at her like she was the funniest stand-up comedian he'd ever heard.

She inched forward and put her SUV in park, got out, and walked into the house with him. "How was dinner with your daughters?" He'd told her more about Kim and Joann on Sunday evening while she brewed up hot chocolate and he popped popcorn. She'd stayed too late, once again making her feel like a much younger woman than she actually was.

"They're great," he said. "Kim has a serious boyfriend. I guess they've started talking about marriage."

"Oh, that's great," she said. "I mean, is that great? Do you like the man she's with?"

"I've never met him," Finn said.

"Oh." Surprise moved through Amanda.

Finn threw her a look as he tossed the mail on the desk and continued to the stovetop, where a pot sat, steam leaking from the lid. He bent and peered into the oven, saying, "A few more minutes. I hope you're not starving."

"I'm fine," she said, taking a spot on the couch across the room. "Are you going to meet the guy before your daughter marries him?"

"I'm sure I will," Finn said, his tone a bit standoffish. "They live an hour away."

"I know," Amanda said. Honestly, was she *trying* to find

a fault in him? Why did she care how he interacted with his daughters? He clearly loved them, and they loved him. "What do you like to do when you're not working around here?"

He got down a couple of plates and faced her. "I like to cross-country ski."

"You're kidding."

"Nope."

"You do that in the winter. You know it's cold in the winter here, right?"

He laughed, making the once-tense atmosphere much lighter. "I know. The trick to enjoying Wyoming is enjoying winter sports."

Amanda felt like someone had poured straight lemon juice down her throat. "I try not to go outside in the winter at all."

"No ice skating?"

"No." She shook her head.

"I suppose ice fishing would be out then." His blue eyes glittered at her all the way from the kitchen, and she wanted to get up and go over there and kiss that mouth.

That cowboy mouth.

"I don't even see the point of fishing when it's warm," she said.

"Oh, boy." He chuckled again. A timer went off, and he turned back to the oven to silence it. He pulled the potatoes out and clicked off the burner under the pot on the stovetop. "I think we're ready."

She joined him in the kitchen, and he folded his arms. "Will you say grace?"

A moment passed between them, and Amanda's body heated in that single breath. "Sure," she said. She thanked the Lord for the food, for the good land where they lived, and asked Him to watch over those they loved. In her heart, she added a silent plea that she could figure out how to make things work with Finn permanently.

She kept those in her heart, though, and after she said, "Amen," he served her a beautiful plate of food.

"You keep doing this, and I won't want to leave."

"That's the point." He grinned at her, but Amanda felt like he'd stabbed her through the heart with his fork.

"Oh?"

He shrugged. "I just want you to know you won't have to take care of me. I can cook, I clean, I do all my own yardwork."

"More than me, then," she said, suddenly remembering she'd brought him a cookie. "Oh, I have something for you." She left her meatballs on the counter and rushed out the front door. Once she'd grabbed it and returned, she held it out to him like she'd brought him the greatest present in the world.

"I bake," she said. "Does that count for something?"

"Sure does," he said, taking the cookie from her. "This is great. You made this from scratch?"

"That's right." She smiled and settled back into her spot beside him at the bar.

"Have you ever wanted to do something different with your life?" he asked. "Open a bakery, that kind of thing?"

She wasn't sure where these questions were coming from, and she filled her mouth with the most delicious meatballs and brown gravy she'd ever had. A moan came out, and he looked at her.

"This is amazing," she said after she'd swallowed. "And no, not really. I mean, I like to bake, but I also like to sleep in."

"Ah, a dangerous combination for a bakery owner," he teased.

"Exactly." The conversation was easy after that, and Amanda stayed for an hour or so. When Finn said he had to get back to work on the farm, rather than go with him, she bid him farewell and got back in her car.

His words about wanting to keep her with him wouldn't leave her mind. As the miles and minutes passed, she realized how different their lives were. They didn't live in the same town. Didn't attend the same church. Didn't even have the same goals.

She wanted a companion. Someone to share her life with. "What does he want?" she asked herself.

If things got serious with them, hard conversations would have to happen. Could she sell her house in Coral Canyon and move to Dog Valley? Live on a farm? Give up her church, her friends, her close proximity to her family?

As the questions tumbled through her mind, Amanda didn't have a concrete answer for any of them. She loved her house in Coral Canyon, and she couldn't imagine selling it. She and Ron had worked so hard on it, and there was so much of both of them there.

She didn't have to decide right now, and she put the thoughts out of her head. They stayed away for approximately four seconds, and then they swirled back to life again.

In the end, she decided to do what she'd once told Eli. "Don't worry so much," she said as she pulled into her garage. "You haven't even kissed him yet. Have fun. Get to know him. Don't worry."

Nodding with utmost determination, she went inside the house. The silent, empty house that she swore one day would swallow her whole.

To ease her loneliness and make the house smaller, she pulled out her phone and texted Finn. *Lunch was delicious. Thank you so much for having me.*

Anytime, Amanda, his response said. *Anytime.*

And looking around the house now, with Finn's words etched in her eyes, she knew she could give up this house. After all, it was just a house, and houses didn't make meatballs in brown gravy or send texts or offer companionship.

Her phone rang, and while she expected it to be Finn, it was Beau.

"Hey, baby," she drawled.

"Ma," he said. "You asked about the cupcake competition, and Lily and I have decided."

"Oh, perfect," she said.

"It'll be a couples competition this time. So you and Finn would work together."

A smile curved her lips. "That's great, son. Just great."

"So you're in?"

"Yes," she said. "Finn and I are in."

"Great. Gotta go," he said, and he hung up before she could even say good-bye. She didn't mind, because all she could think about now was seeing Finn in an apron, trying to fill or frost a cupcake.

She couldn't wait for the Whiskey Mountain Lodge Cupcake Wars. Oh, no, she could not.

CHAPTER 12

F inn reached for the thistle that was trying to hide back behind the rose bush, sweat dripping down his face. As much as he loved summer, he could do without Mother Nature trying to bake the state of Wyoming off the face of the planet.

His garden sure did like it though, and his sprinkling system had come on that morning, so the ground was nice and wet for weeding. He'd been fitting in little tasks like getting the flowerbeds around his trees cleared in any spot of time he could find.

Now that he was dating Amanda, spending time with her had taken priority over some things. They'd been out a few more times over the past couple of weeks, and she still slipped through her front door with a coy smile on her face before he could kiss her.

Every dang time.

Finn wasn't sure what kind of signal she was trying to send. He should probably just ask her. Get it out in the open. It wasn't like he had to hide how he felt about her.

With the weeding done along the side of the house where he had a dozen rose bushes standing sentinel, he retreated to the front steps, which were bathed in late afternoon shade.

His thumbs hovered over the screen, but in the end, he tapped to her name and hit the green phone button to call her. She didn't have a paying job, but Finn had learned over the last few weeks that she spent plenty of time working. She helped people from her church. She babysat her grandkids. She baked things and took them to people who couldn't get out of their homes, or who needed a pick-me-up.

She did a few things around her yard, but she paid a gardener to do the bulk of the care, and Finn was actually considering doing the same thing.

"Hey," she said, her voice bright and cheerful on the other end of the line. "What's up?"

"Hey," he said, his mind suddenly blank as to why he'd called. The Cupcake Wars at Graham's lodge was a couple of days away, and that was the next time he'd been planning to see her.

"Are you going to make me try to read your mind?" she teased.

"No." He cleared his throat. "Okay, I have a question for you. It's a yes-no type of deal. I really only need one word. I don't need an explanation or anything."

A beat of silence passed. "Finn, I'm a little worried right now, I'm not going to lie."

"I'm scared out of my mind," he said, wondering what on Earth had possessed him to call. "It's just...we've been out several times now. You hold my hand. You seem to have a good time. I walk you to the door...and you slip away. Is that what we are? Don't answer that; that's not the question." He drew in a deep breath.

"Are you ever going to let me kiss you?" he asked.

A healthy amount of silence poured through the line before Amanda started laughing. "That's the question?"

"A yes or no would suffice," he said, feeling more and more foolish as she continued giggling.

"Yes," she said.

Relief rushed through him. "All right. That's all I had."

"That's it?"

"Yep."

"What are you doing tonight?" she asked.

"I've got a meeting tonight, remember? That guy from—"

"Spirit Lake," they said together. "I remember," she added.

"I'll see you at the lodge on Saturday, though," he said. "Right?"

"Right. You've been practicing your frosting making skills?"

"Uh," Finn said. "I think that was on my agenda for tomorrow."

That got her to laugh again, and Finn smiled at the

sound of it coursing through his ears. The call ended, and he sat on the front steps for a few more minutes, just enjoying the country air, the stillness of his farm—and the fact that he was going to get to kiss Amanda Whittaker at some point in the future.

SATURDAY AFTERNOON FOUND him pulling into the parking lot at Whiskey Mountain Lodge. He'd been inside a time or two, but usually just to hover near the front door while Beau got something for him. He spent a lot more time down the road at the ranch Laney and Graham owned, so he wasn't quite used to the grandeur that awaited him inside the lodge.

And the noise.

"You made it," Amanda said with a smile after she'd opened the front door.

"I made it." He held up his apron. "And this came in the mail this morning, so I'm ready."

She laughed, embraced him, and said, "We're waiting in the kitchen. Come on."

There were easily twenty adults in the kitchen and dining room, which were connected to make one big space. The kitchen was large, but there was no way ten couples could create cupcakes in there. He slipped a half-step behind Amanda easily, hoping no one would look his way.

However, it felt like every eye in the place had locked onto him, and he couldn't help squirming and shifting a little bit.

Finally, a woman waved both arms above her head, and said, "It's time to begin. Everyone quiet down."

"That's Celia Armstrong," Amanda said, leaning her head close to his. "She's the chef here at the lodge, and she organizes these cupcake events."

Finn felt like he needed to get a new job, because organizing cupcake events sounded a heck of a lot more fun than walking through the henhouse to gather eggs. It smelled astronomically better, he knew that.

"We're working in teams of two today," she said. "Two couples will battle up here, while two battle downstairs. The winner from upstairs will go against the winner from downstairs, and we'll have one champion per round." She glanced around at the crowd. "I believe we had eight couples signed up, but I don't see Vi…."

"She's coming," Lily said. "She'll be here in time for round two."

Finn was glad he knew a few faces and names, at least.

Celia nodded while saying, "Then the two winners from each round will do one last bake. A quick bake. One cupcake. Their best cupcake. A winner will be named from that bake-off." She turned and lifted a whiteboard onto the counter. "I've got the brackets here. Come see when and where you're baking. The first round will begin in ten minutes."

Chatter broke out again, and several people surged toward the white board. Amanda slipped her hand into his as a few people turned toward them. "Ready?" she asked, but Finn didn't have any time to answer before a man who looked very much like Graham said, "I'm Andrew, Amanda's son."

"Hello," Finn said, putting on his best smile. "I'm Finley Barber."

"Andrew is married to Becca," Amanda said, though she'd rehearsed this information to him before. "They have a daughter Chrissy, and—"

"And this is my baking partner today," Andrew practically yelled, grabbing onto a dark-haired woman. "Bree. She's our gardener here, but Celia's been giving her some baking lessons, and I think we're going to take this trophy home today."

"Oh, please," Amanda said. "Last time I checked, you ate out for every meal."

Bree laughed, and Finn did too, though he wasn't much better. He could make a few things, and he could definitely read and follow a recipe. He hadn't practiced any frostings, but how hard could they be?

"You're up in the first round, Mom," Graham said, tying an apron around his waist. "Hey, Finn."

"Graham."

"I hope you brought your A-game," he said with a glint in his eyes. "Laney and I have been practicing for weeks, and you're up against us."

"Upstairs or down?" Amanda asked, stepping away from Finn but not removing her hand from his. He went with her, somewhat surprised at the smack talk happening in this family. He actually enjoyed it, and it made them all seem more human. More real. More enjoyable to be around.

"Upstairs," Graham said.

"She can't measure flour right now," Amanda called, and Celia whipped around from the white board to reprimand Laney.

Finn started laughing, and Amanda smiled in a predatory way. "We're going to cream you," she said to Graham. "Come on, Finn. Let's strategize."

He wasn't sure what there was to strategize about, but he said hello to a few more people as Amanda tugged him into the kitchen. He tied on his apron, and he listened to her talk about making a churro cupcake and a triple chocolate cupcake.

He literally would be making fillings and frostings, and he told her he could do it. Because he could. He could whip butter and powdered sugar to make buttercream. He could melt chocolate and pour it into molds. Everything she detailed for him, her mouth moving so fast he could barely see it, he could do.

She'd make the cupcakes and get them in the oven before making the churros. They'd decorate together, though Finn knew that meant he'd stick a sugared churro in the frosting after she piped it onto the cupcake.

"Two minutes," Celia called. "If you're not in this round, you have to leave the kitchen." She walked out of the dining room and a moment later, yelled the same thing downstairs.

Finn felt an energy in his soul he hadn't in a long, long time.

"Go!" Celia yelled, and Amanda thrust the recipes at him and flew into motion. He moved a little slower, getting out all the ingredients he needed for both frostings and the two fillings before beginning. He'd start with the chocolate pudding, so it could set up. Then he'd do the cinnamon sugar butter for the churro cupcake. Then frostings, as those really were just whip-it-together type of things.

He worked in a small area, only needing one burner and a mixer on the counter. Chaos reigned around him, but he focused on his tasks. Amanda kept checking with him, but all he could say was, "I'm on schedule, sweetheart," or "Everything's great. We're going to win this."

She seemed to be a Tasmanian devil in the kitchen, and he wanted to just sit and watch her work. She was breathtakingly beautiful, and Finn felt himself slipping toward falling in love with her.

By the time Amanda said, "I need the pudding, Finn," it was chilled and ready. He pulled it out of the fridge and handed it to her.

"Tell me what to do to help," he said.

"Use this to take out a chunk of cupcake from the churro ones," she said, handing him a tool that looked like an apple corer. He did as she said, pulling out little nuggets of cupcake from four vanilla-cinnamon cakes.

"Put in the cinnamon butter," she said as she pressed her piping tip up into the chocolate cupcakes and squeezed in the pudding.

He carefully scooped out little round balls of cinnamon-sugar butter and placed them in the center of the cupcakes.

"Piping bags?" he asked, already reaching for one.

"Yes, please."

He loaded them both—one with the white chocolate frosting he'd made and one with the cinnamon frosting—and handed her the chocolate one as soon as she set down the pudding. She swirled beautiful mountains of frosting on the cupcake and said, "Garnish."

Finn went back to the fridge as Celia called, "Two minutes, people! Two minutes. All cupcakes have to be in the judging spot in two minutes." He almost tripped over his own feet, but he managed to open the fridge and retrieve the cowboy boots he'd made from semi-sweet and bittersweet chocolate.

"Finn, pull those churros out, would you?" Amanda sounded near panic.

Finn left the chocolate on the counter, and using a pair of tongs, removed the short churro sticks from the hot oil on the stove. She had a plate of cinnamon and sugar sitting there, and he placed the fried dough on it. With his hands, he quickly rolled them around, getting them covered.

Moving back to the cowboy boots, he carefully stuck one in each mound of frosting and put three cupcakes on a long, white plate Amanda had ready for him. "These are done, sweetheart."

"Take them to judging," she said, finishing the last swirl on the churro cupcake. "These are too hot." She grabbed the churros and tossed them on a clean plate, sticking that in the freezer while Finn took their first plate of triple chocolate cupcakes to the a taped-off area on the dining room table.

Celia grinned at him, and while he didn't know her, he smiled right on back. "Thirty seconds!" she called.

Finn spun back to the kitchen, noticing Graham and Laney had all their cupcakes in the judging square already. "Gonna have to take them out," he told her.

"Ten more seconds." Amanda looked like she'd swallowed a beehive as she turned and put the three best churro cakes on the plate. It felt like ten years passed before she yanked open the freezer and stabbed the churro sticks in the top of the frosting, making them look like perfect little teacups with straws.

She dashed over to the table and put the plate down just as Celia said, "Time's up!"

Amanda threw up her hands and laughed, turning to Finn and grabbing him in a tight hug. "Nice job, cowboy," she said, making his every cell light up.

"Judges," Celia said, and several children entered the dining room. "This is a blind taste test. The kids don't know who made what cupcake."

Finn stood there with his arm around Amanda, more nervous than he thought he'd be. For some reason, he really wanted to win. For her. So she'd be proud of him.

They tried all the cupcakes and whispering ensued. Celia bent down with all of them, finally straightening and saying, "The children have chosen the triple chocolate cupcake and the churro cupcake as the winners."

Amanda shrieked, throwing both hands up into the air again. She hugged Finn before taking a few steps and hugging her son and daughter-in-law too. Finn shook both of their hands, and though he'd lost, Graham couldn't seem to stop smiling.

"Good job, Finn," he said, taking off his apron. "Come on, Laney, let's go get some ice cream down at the ranch." They left the kitchen, and Amanda nodded toward a doorway.

Finn followed her, a happiness making his steps light as they went into the backyard. "That was incredible," he said.

"Yeah?" she asked, turning back to him. "You enjoyed it?"

"So much fun." He gathered her into his arms. "And we won. I told you I wouldn't let you down." With that, he bent his head toward her, finally going to get his kiss.

And what a kiss. Her lips tasted like chocolate and cinnamon, and Finn's mouth fit against hers so well, she felt made to kiss him.

She pressed into him, taking the kiss one step further, and he went with her, his heartbeat pounding and every sense on high alert. It didn't matter that the sun was so dang hot. Didn't matter that his hands were still sticky with sugar and icing. Nothing mattered in that moment but kissing Amanda.

So Finn focused on that.

CHAPTER 13

Amanda held onto Finn's face, the heat spiraling through her body absolutely lethal. Pure pleasure wove through her, and she kissed Finn like her life depended on having her lips on his.

He finally pulled away, and Amanda sighed, immediately sucking at the air again. "Wow," she said, tucking herself against his chest.

Finn said nothing, but held her against his pulse, and she'd never felt safer than she did in his arms. She wasn't sure why she'd slid away from him after all those dates, but after he'd called a couple of days ago, she hadn't been able to stop thinking about it.

The only reason she could come up with was Jason. And she hated that. But Jason had never let her slip away from him. He'd have said, "Can you stay here for a second? I want to kiss you."

And then he'd have done it.

Finn wasn't Jason, and Amanda knew it. Jason kissed her like he wanted her, but Finn kissed her like he loved her. There was a distinct difference, and while she wanted to be wanted *and* loved, she was glad Finn's kiss had held more adoration than passion. At least for now.

"So we have an hour," he said. "Want to show me around this place?"

"Sure," she said, stepping out of his arms and linking her arm through his. "We sit out here and eat on Sundays sometimes. The kids like to play in the pool or on the swings. My older granddaughter likes to ride horses."

"Ah, so she's a cowgirl." Finn chuckled.

"A little bit, yeah," Amanda said. "It's Graham's step-daughter, Bailey."

"She's definitely a cowgirl," Finn said. "I like her. She's a good girl."

Amanda led him down the sidewalk toward the stables. "I don't come down here much, but it seems like your territory. Beau takes care of the horses here. There's a dozen or so."

"Any other animals?"

"A couple of dogs, maybe." Amanda turned him toward the forest. "There's a nice path back here." They entered the shade, and the temperature went down a few degrees, thankfully. "You were great in the kitchen. So calm."

"We better talk about what we're going to do in the bake-off," he said. "I'm not sure I'm ready for that. Sounds like it'll be a fast round."

"It's thirty minutes," she said. "We should do mini cupcakes. They'll bake faster. We can't do a filling, but we could dip in a ganache or something."

"A gan-what?"

Amanda laughed, clinging to Finn as if she couldn't walk on her own. She felt like a flirty schoolgirl as she said, "It's just a chocolate sauce. That will protect the frosting from melting too badly."

"So we know the judges are kids…chocolate chip cupcakes?"

"That's a great idea," Amanda said. "In the cake batter and the frosting." They walked under the trees, the scene serene and quiet, and Amanda breathed in deeply, a measure of peace moving through her.

"I love these mountains," she said.

"They're beautiful," Finn said. "Not many mountains where I'm from in Kentucky."

"Not many in Texas either." The stroll calmed her, and she turned back to the lodge. "We should get back. I bet we'll have to go up against Bree and Andrew." She started back along the path, and Finn moved his hand to hers.

At the edge of the trees, she paused, wanting another kiss before she had to go back inside and bake her way to victory. Finn seemed to be able to read her mind, because he brought her close and touched his lips to hers for just a moment before growling and claiming her mouth as his.

She never wanted to kiss another man again. Only him. Only Finn.

❦

LATER, she stood in the kitchen, sweating as she watched the children taste the cupcakes on the table. They had gone up against Andrew and Bree, and Bree had somehow made a caramel apple cake in only thirty minutes. With candied apples and a caramel frosting, the cupcake looked delicious.

Their chocolate chip cookie dough cupcake didn't seem as impressive, and she couldn't tell how the judges felt about it. The whispered conversation seemed to go on and on, and she thought she might squeeze off Finn's hand before the winner was announced.

Celia finally beamed at the kids and looked at Amanda, Finn, Andrew, and Bree, who stood in the kitchen as if the cash award for this Cupcake Wars was substantial. The other participating couples loitered around too, and the tension in the lodge could've been cut with a knife.

"And the winner is...Bree and Andrew!" The kids cheered, and disappointment cut through Amanda. But she grinned and hugged her son and Bree before stepping over to the table to try their cupcake.

It was salty and sweet, and her eyes nearly rolled back in her head at the deliciousness of it. "This is so good," she said around her mouthful of treat. "No wonder they won."

Finn approached her, a smile on his face. "We tried."

"We sure did."

"I'm starving for something without sugar," he said. "Want to go to dinner with me?"

They'd driven separately, but she could drive down the canyon and go to dinner with him. "Sure. What did you have in mind?"

"Nothing fancy. Just a boring steakhouse or something."

"Want me to cook?" Amanda started combing through her memory for what she could possibly make for them. "I can make a mean skillet lasagna in a half an hour."

"Your place?" he asked, the interest in his expression off the charts. Amanda imagined kissing him in her kitchen, on the back deck.

"Yep," she said, popping the P.

"I'll meet you down there," he said. "I'll stop and get something to drink. Sound good?"

"Sure. Let me say good-bye to my kids."

"Take your time." He reached in his pocket and withdrew his keys. "I'll see you in a bit." He started for the front door, and she went with him, not daring to kiss him in front of the few people sitting on the couch in the living room.

She'd just turned around to find Celia and thank her for the fun Cupcake War and to say good-bye to her family when Beau approached.

"Ma," he said. "Nice job in the kitchen. I'm sure you deserved to win."

"No." She shook her head. "Did you taste that caramel apple cupcake? It was amazing."

"And you and Finn? Looked like you were plenty *sympatico* while making cupcakes...." He grinned at her, but Amanda had never discussed her dating life with her kids. She kept things neutral, letting her actions show her feelings for a particular man.

"He's a good man," she said. "Thanks for setting us up."

"That was Graham," Beau said, holding up both his hands. "I mean, maybe I suggested him, but Graham did all the contacting and arranging."

"Well, we're getting along," Amanda said. "Give your mother a hug. I'm leaving."

Beau engulfed her in a big bear hug, and Amanda laughed. "Bye, Ma."

"Love you, Beau. Tell your brothers good-bye for me. Kiss your wife. Squeeze Charlie." She smiled and headed for the door. The silence in her SUV felt heavenly, and she basked in it for a few moments before starting the engine and adjusting the air conditioning.

She beat Finn to her house and started getting out ingredients. The past month flowed through her mind, and she paused as the ground beef sizzled in the pan. What would life be like with him in it permanently? If she'd been home when the buyer from Spirit Lake came, and if she had to arrange her schedule to fit his, or tell him exactly what she did and where she went all day.

He didn't seem like the controlling type, and her thoughts weren't negative. She was simply seeing if she had room for that type of commitment in her life. Not that she needed to make it right now, though she certainly wasn't getting any younger.

The doorbell chimed, startling her. She looked frantically toward the front of the house, though she couldn't see the door from here, and back to the pan of ground beef she'd started and had done nothing with. It snapped angrily now, and she flipped the knob to turn off the flame.

Feeling giddy for a reason she couldn't name, she pulled open the front door, almost throwing herself in Finn's arms. But he held a fountain drink in one hand and a case of strawberry lemonade in the other.

"They had that Lemonhead brand you like," he said, lifting it up with a smile.

"Come on in." She held onto the door as she stepped back, a glow spreading through her when he walked in.

He whistled as he looked up at the vaulted ceilings and around at the lobby. Amanda knew the house was a little ridiculous. But she'd raised four teenage boys here, and she'd always dreamed of having them bring their families here, stay the night, fill the walls with laughter again.

Then Ron had died, and Graham had bought the lodge. That had become the epicenter of Whittaker family events, as every son had lived there, every son had fallen in love there. Every Christmas was spent there, and Amanda had made peace with it.

Sometimes she kept a grandchild overnight, but not

often. Now, when Eli and Meg came to town, they stayed at the lodge. Amanda's heart pinched, because she knew she didn't need to hang onto this house, but she wasn't sure she could give it up.

"Nice place," he said.

"Thank you," she said simply. She walked past her army of plants that welcomed everyone to her home, and went into the kitchen. "You can put the lemonade in the fridge if you want," she said.

He did as she turned the flame back on and turned to chop an onion. His arms came around her from behind, causing goosebumps to erupt over her arms. She smiled, sighed, and sagged back into him.

"You really don't have to cook," he murmured, his lips skating down the side of her neck. "If you're too tired, let's order something."

She wanted to do exactly that. Kiss him until she didn't have to think about selling her house, or the death of her husband, or Whiskey Mountain Lodge.

Setting down the knife, she turned in his arms and kissed him, the union almost frantic at first. He pulled away and looked at her. "What's wrong?"

"Nothing."

"Amanda," he said, concern filling those blue eyes now. "You were okay when I left you at the lodge. Did something happen?"

She shook her head, unable to look at him any longer. She ducked her head and tucked herself against his chest. "I'm fine. Just thinking about some things."

And she really needed to stir that meat or turn off the burner.

"What kind of things?" Finn asked. "Maybe I can help."

She disentangled herself from him and moved back to the stove. "Ron and I built this house so we could have our family here as it grew and expanded." She didn't look at him as she returned to the cutting board. She made quick work of the onion as she said, "I sometimes have one of my sons here, or a single grandchild, but it's not the family meeting place I imagined it would be." She glanced at him but couldn't hold his gaze for long. "Sometimes it upsets me a little bit that Graham bought the lodge, and everyone gathers there. That's all."

"Understandable," Finn said.

She turned and dropped the onions into the pan, stirring them around. "We eat there every Sunday. There's a huge shin-dig at Thanksgiving and Christmas, though it's really Christmas that takes the cake at the lodge." She tried to smile, but it wasn't as easy as she'd like it to be.

"Ron died just after Christmas," she whispered. Trying to gather her emotions back into the box where she kept them, she lifted her head high and moved to the pantry to get the homemade tomato sauce and a bag of pasta.

"I only have campanelle," she said when she came back. Finn hadn't moved, and he watched her with guarded eyes. "Hope that's okay."

"I don't even know what that is," he said, his tone trying to be playful and failing.

"It's a little cone-shaped pasta," she said, ripping open the bag and taking one out. "It's got a ruffled edge, see?"

"I'm sure it'll be fine," he said.

"It holds the meat and sauce pretty well."

"Great."

Amanda was aware she was avoiding the conversation, but she didn't care. She didn't want tonight to be heavy, not after a great afternoon and a spectacular kiss. She poured in the tomato sauce, satisfied at the instant boil, and added the pasta, stirring everything around.

With a lid on the pan and a timer set for ten minutes, she turned back to Finn. "I'm fine, Finn," she said. "I don't want to dwell on unhappy things tonight, okay?"

"Okay," he said.

"What's in the cup?" She nodded toward it. "I didn't realize you were a big soda drinker."

A smile danced across his lips. "Oh, I love the stuff."

"Is that right?" she asked, warmth filling her chest. Having him in her house felt intimate and…right, and she was so glad he was there.

"Yeah," he said. "Tell me something about you I don't know yet."

Wanting to keep things light between them, she moved over to a drawer on the same side of the counter as the stove. "This is my spice drawer." She opened it. "I labeled it."

"Labeled it?" He joined her, bringing the delicious scent of cologne and chocolate with him. Peering into the drawer, he said, "Oh, wow."

"I might have an unhealthy relationship with my label maker." She laughed, the sound and action freeing up some of the tension in her chest.

Finn's slow, passionate kiss broke up the rest, and Amanda finally relaxed in his arms.

She'd save the heavy conversations for later. Tonight was about her and Finn—and a bubbling skillet of lasagna.

CHAPTER 14

Fireworks exploded overhead, and Finn's whole body felt like someone had shoved a sparkler inside him. He'd spent the day with Amanda, first at a parade in Coral Canyon, then at a family picnic up at the lodge. She didn't seem upset that the event wasn't at her place, but he could easily see how it could be.

Her house was as large as the lodge, without as many bedrooms upstairs. More shared living spaces, which would actually be conducive to having a large group of adults around. But he said nothing. He appreciated that she'd opened up to him, and the weeks since had been filled with fun text conversations, random lunch dates, and loads of kissing.

Oh, yes, Finn really liked Amanda. They weren't moving very fast, but he was too old for such things anyway.

They'd gone to dinner alone, but then they'd met her family at the rodeo grounds for the fireworks. She'd been entertaining Ronnie for most of the evening, and she held the little boy on her lap now during the show.

Finn liked the way she leaned into him as she looked up into the sky. He liked holding her hand. He liked the orange and rose scent of her hair. He liked the way her lips felt against his, and he liked having someone to share his life with.

They'd been seeing each other for nearly two months now, and he felt like his simple life had been laid out on paper pretty early on. He didn't have a lot of surprises to reveal, other than things he did for his job, and Amanda had been a little shocked to learn he organized and ran a jockey training camp in August.

Only a month away, and he was seriously behind in his preparations for it. He'd secured a location months ago, and he'd been watching the registrations. They'd filled last week, and he had a healthy waiting list now, too.

He'd done the camp before, but there was plenty to prepare each time, and he needed to dig into that soon. Very soon.

The music crescendoed around him, and the sky filled with dazzling lights and pops and bombs. It seemed to go on for a very long time, and then the crowd cheered loudly.

"All done," Amanda said to Ronnie, pure happiness on her face. Finn didn't have grandchildren yet, but he could plainly see how much she loved hers. "Go sit with Finny for a second, Ronnie. Grandma needs to get your stuff." She passed the little boy to Finn, who froze with the child on his lap.

A moment later, everything relaxed. He could hold a three-year-old. The boy didn't even know him, but he sank into him, his fist clutched around a glow-in-the-dark stick. "What color is it?" he asked the boy, who turned and looked up at him.

"Green," he said.

Finn smiled at him. "Good boy." He hadn't been to a fireworks show in a long time. He never set them off at home either, as the Labs didn't like the loud noises. The horses either. Finn barely tolerated them. But tonight, as he watched families clean up and start heading down the aisles, a sense of wonder and joy filled him.

Life was meant to be lived—outside the walls of his home and the fences on his farm. Sure, he loved those things, but he could have more. He loved spending time with Amanda and her family, and he realized in that moment that if things progressed with them, and they got married, he'd be taking on the entire Whittaker family. Four new sons. Four new daughters-in-law. Six grandchildren and counting.

And he wanted them all.

"I'll take him," Laney said, breaking into Finn's thoughts as she bent to pick up her son. "Come on, buddy. It's way past bedtime."

He held up his toy. "Green, Mama."

"I know. It's green." She flashed a smile at Finn and added, "It's good to see you, Finn."

"You too, Laney." She moved out into the aisle behind Graham, and Finn stood up too. He folded the blanket he'd been sitting on and tucked it under his arm.

"Ready?" he asked Amanda. He'd driven to her place, and she'd had her SUV loaded up with blankets and a cooler.

"Yep." He stepped out into the aisle and waited for her to go in front of him. They battled the crowds, something Finn usually didn't appreciate. But tonight, holding Amanda's hand, everything was fine.

Back at her place, he helped her carry in the cooler and stack all the unopened bottles of water and cans of soda in her fridge. He took the ice out to the backyard and dumped it out before turning the cooler upside down and leaving it propped against the bottom step of the deck.

Returning the house, he found Amanda holding a small box wrapped in silver paper. "What's going on?" he asked, his step slowing.

"I saw this and thought of you," she said, a smile covering up some of her exhaustion.

"I don't have anything for you." He approached slowly, feeling somewhat foolish.

"A return gift is not required." She handed him the box, and it was lighter than he'd imagined it would be. His mind raced as he lifted the top of the box off to peer inside.

A packet of seeds sat there. He grinned and looked at Amanda. "What is this?"

"Take them out."

He did, but they weren't the kind of seeds he would buy at the nursery, and they didn't come in a fancy, labeled package. They came with earth attached, and he quickly realized they were bulbs, not seeds.

"Amanda." He didn't meant to say her name with so much reverence. So much...love. It just happened. "You didn't just find these. You had to go looking." He met her eyes, finding the truth there. "Where did you get them?"

"Did you know there's only a few places that will ship bulbs out?" She grinned at him. "And it should be above freezing for the required time if you plant them now."

Since the package bore no writing, he had no idea what color they'd be. "Thank you," he said. "I know right where to put these."

"I know you do." She took them from him and set the bulbs back in the box. "You told me all about it a few weeks ago as you took me on a tour of your yard." She put herself in his arms and stretched up to kiss him.

Finn kissed her back, a new thrill entering his bloodstream. "Thank you," he murmured against her lips before claiming them again. He couldn't help wondering if her giving him something to grow on his land meant she'd come live with him if they got married.

He couldn't believe he was thinking about marriage again, but his mind seemed to go where it wanted to go. They had a lot to discuss to merge their two lives, but in that moment, late at night on the Fourth of July, he just kissed Amanda—and that was enough for now.

🌼

WEEKS PASSED, and he saw her a little bit less than he would've liked. But summer was a busy time on the farm, and he had the jockey training camp to prep for. He worked from sunup to sundown, and the only times he saw Amanda in the flesh were when she brought food to his house for dinner, or they met for a quick lunch in Dog Valley.

The day before the camp, he was supposed to take Amanda to dinner, but his phone rang that morning, the name of a past client on the screen.

"Jimmer," Finn said, pleasantly surprised.

"Finn," the man said. "I heard you have a colt that's ready to run."

"Do I?" Finn asked, not sure who Jimmer had been talking to.

"Always Boss," he said. "The dam was Trophy Bound."

Finn loved it when clients came to him, as hunting down a buyer for a horse was one of the hardest and least-liked part of what he did. "That's right," Finn said. "Sire was All Or Nothing."

"I want him," Jimmer said.

"You haven't even seen him," Finn argued. "I've got jockey camp tomorrow. I'll be back midweek. Come out to the farm—"

"I'm in town," Jimmer said. "I can be there by this evening."

Surprise lifted Finn's eyebrows. "You want to see him run tonight?"

"Is he ready?"

"He has great game," Finn said. "Good for me as groom."

"I want to see him tonight," Jimmer said. "I'll be there around six."

Finn agreed, because he didn't see a way around it. Jimmer VanGuard was one of the biggest names in horseracing, and if Finn could sell Almost Boss that night? He'd do it.

He sent a quick text to Amanda, knowing she'd be disappointed. Heck, he was disappointed. But he pulled his boots on and headed out to the farm, because there was work to do, and sometimes he didn't get everything in his life that he wanted.

That evening, Jimmer showed up promptly at six. Finn had only gotten one text from Amanda, and it said, *Dang. We'll go when you get back,* and he'd taken it to mean she wasn't too terribly upset.

He'd set aside a couple of things that day that his temporary help could finish up tomorrow in order to be ready to show Jimmer the horse. He rattled off facts about the dam and sire as he led the potential buyer out to the corral.

Only Almost Boss stood there, and he was tall and dark and beautiful. Jimmer's face didn't so much as twitch. Finn detailed the training the horse had, and how much he still had to complete. "But you've got Jute, and he'll be great with Almost Boss," he said.

"I want you," Jimmer said, his eyes staying on the horse.

Finn squinted at him. "Me? What?"

Jimmer finally swung his gaze to Finn. "I want you to be the horse's trainer."

"I can't do that," Finn said immediately, shaking his head. "I don't travel the circuit, and I have five other horses here to work with. My farm." He definitely would not be leaving all of that. "What happened to Jute?"

Jimmer's face darkened, and Finn knew he wasn't used to getting told no. "He found a better offer," he said roughly.

"I can get you some names," he said.

"I don't need names." Jimmer sighed and knocked on the top of the fence. "Let's see 'im run."

Finn didn't like the way this man demanded everything from him, but he could potentially make a lot of money tonight. So he jumped the fence and approached the colt. "Hey, boy," he said, putting his hand right on the animal's nose. "Let's show him what you've got, okay? Ready to run for me?"

He led the horse toward the gate, relieved and satisfied when he plodded along, his head bobbing right beside Finn's shoulder the way he'd been trained.

They went over to the practice track Finn had carefully measured, leveled, and maintained for exactly such a purpose. He trained horses to blind start, come out of gates, take off with a bell, all of it. He trained them to ride high on corners or stick close to the railing. He loved everything about horseracing, except actually attending any of the events. He'd wanted to be a trainer since childhood but working for his father had spoiled that.

Pushing those thoughts aside, he saddled Almost Boss with the jockey saddle as if he were really going to race. He didn't put blinders on, as the horse hadn't really raced against another yet, and he hadn't truly developed his racing personality.

"All right," he told the horse. "He might buy you if you show him what you've got. Give him your best game, all right?" Of course the horse didn't know what Finn was telling him, but he understood the steps Finn had gone through. He was in racing mode, and Finn stepped out of the racetrack and over to the bell switch.

"Ready?" he asked Jimmer, who nodded. He flipped the switch and watched with pride as Almost Boss ran.

He went once around the track and started a second lap. Before he'd reached the curve, Jimmer said, "I'll take 'im."

"You don't even know how much he is."

"I'll take 'im," Jimmer repeated, glaring at Finn as he turned. "I'll be back up here in a couple of months. Do you think you can start working with him with a jockey?"

"Do you have someone in mind?"

"I'll send up Kent," he said, walking away and leaving Finn to take care of Almost Boss. He did, excitement building in him as he brushed down the horse and returned him to the stable.

"He bought you," he said, stroking the colt's mane. "And he's sending Kent, who's a great rider. I just know you're going to win everything someday." He loved his horses, and he wanted to celebrate that he'd found Almost Boss a good home, even if Jimmer was a bit prickly.

Kent wasn't, and if they could find the right trainer for Almost Boss, the horse's potential was unlimited.

He returned to the house, needing to call Amanda and tell her his good news. It was strange and wonderful that he wanted to share his life with her and only her, but he did.

So he made the call, his voice animated and loud when he said, "Guess what? I sold Almost Boss tonight," instead of hello.

CHAPTER 15

Amanda missed Finn while he was out of town. She somehow felt his presence leave the state, and she couldn't help pining for him until he came back.

He texted her often from his jockey camp in California, where he did training and education at the racetrack in Santa Ana.

Amanda had been to California a few times over the years to visit Eli and Meg, who lived in a tiny cottage near the beach. She loved the ocean, but not as much as the mountains, and Wyoming always drew her home again.

Finn returned after his training days in California, and he somehow looked tanner than she remembered. His voice was deeper. His smile brighter. She felt like running to him as she approached the house and he stood from where he'd been sitting in a chair on the porch.

She giggled as she threw her arms around him. "You're

back." She tipped up on her toes, glad his strong hands held onto her waist and steadied her as she met his lips with hers.

"Mm," he said, molding his mouth to her and kissing her.

The wind whispered around them, and the scent of roses hung heavily in the air. Amanda enjoyed the muskier notes from Finn's skin, and the mint and chocolate taste of his mouth. She pulled away, a grin permanently on her face now that he was home. "Did you have ice cream for breakfast?"

"Guilty," he said, chuckling. "Hey, I've got to enjoy it while it's warm."

"It's hot," she said.

"You won't be complaining about that in about a month," he said, touching his lips to the corner of her eye, then her earlobe. She leaned into his touch, fire racing through her whole body.

"Do you want to come to church with me this week?" she whispered.

Finn stilled, and Amanda's tension increased too. "Church? With you in Coral Canyon?"

"That's right." She stayed right in his arms but pulled back to look up at him. "I could come with you the week after that."

Finn looked thoughtful, and she suspected she knew what he was thinking about. She couldn't quite give a voice to it yet, but she'd been thinking about merging their lives together. She'd never had to think like this with the other men she'd dated. They lived in the same town, and none of them had minded switching to her church, sitting beside her on the bench.

But Dog Valley was much too far away for Finn to drive every day. And he couldn't give up his farm.

"I think...." she started, unsure how to finish. "I think if we're going to keep seeing each other—and I want to do that—we should be thinking a little bit down the road," she said, the words coming to her the moment she said them.

"What are you thinking about that road?" he asked, falling back a step and taking her hand in his. "Let's go inside while we talk. You've got to try this ice cream."

She smiled to herself as she followed him, and she let him start to scoop up some bright green ice cream with chocolate chunks in it. "I'm thinking that if we get married, we'll need a plan for things."

"What kind of things?" he asked, and Amanda was grateful he hadn't freaked out about the word *marriage*.

She was surprised she'd brought it up, actually. She usually waited a lot longer than this to broach the subject, and she and Finn had only been dating for a few months. Of course, she'd only dated a couple of men longer than him, and she and Jason had talked about marriage for two years before she'd finally broken up with him.

A sense of missing she didn't understand pulled through her. Why Jason was still in her heart, she didn't know. She knew they weren't meant to be together. And the kind, hardworking, handsome cowboy in front of her felt good, and right, and wonderful.

"Where we'll live, for one," she said. "And that influences everything else." She watched him, seeing the stutter in his movement as he reached for the silverware drawer. He got out a spoon and put it in the treat before bringing it to her.

"It's pistachio mint chocolate chip."

"Thank you." She smiled up at him and patted the couch cushion next to her. "What do you think? Have you thought very far down the road?"

"Of course I have, Amanda," he said quietly, studying the floor and hanging his hands between his knees.

"And?" she pressed.

"And I feel like you'd have to give up everything you've had for forty-five years to be my wife." He looked at her openly then, his eyes showing his vulnerability. "And I'm not ready to ask you to do that."

His words punched the air out of her lungs. She hadn't thought of it in such harsh terms. *Give up everything she'd had for forty-five years.*

When he put it like that....

She nodded, her throat closing in on itself. She put a bite of ice cream in her mouth anyway, the chill of it shocking her again. "Mm," she said as the sweetness took over. "This is fantastic."

"I'd want to keep my farm," he continued as if she hadn't spoken. "I'm not ready to retire, and this is my living. Which means you'd have to move here. Give up your church, your friends, your house...."

"I understand," she said, just to get him to stop talking. She smiled at him, but it wobbled on her face. "At least we're both thinking about it."

And she wouldn't have to give up her family. It was just a longer drive to the lodge from Dog Valley than it was from her house in town. She ate the rest of her ice cream in silence, and while she and Finn hadn't needed to fill every moment with conversation, this quietness gnawed at her nerves.

"Are we at an impasse?" he asked from beside her.

She looked at him, trying to figure out the threads of feelings running through her. "I don't think so. I sure like you, and I want you to come to church with me this Sunday." She could think that far ahead, and she hadn't seen anything about Finn that required them to break up.

Finn smiled, the gesture so gentle and strong at the same time. "I can do that."

"Starts at ten."

"I'll see if I can pull myself out of bed that early."

Amanda giggled, got up, and said, "Take me out to the barn and show me something I don't know about."

Finn took her bowl into the kitchen. "Really?"

"Really." She clasped her hand in his, thinking that if she was even going to consider living on this farm, she better get to know it a little better than she currently did.

AMANDA PUT the last cinnamon stick in the slow cooker, the final touch on the hot apple cider she and Finn would enjoy after church. She had the potatoes peeled and soaking in water already, and she'd made a raspberry gelatin dessert that morning already as well. She'd put the short ribs in the pressure cooker after church, and they'd eat like kings—and drink hot apple cider as the weather seemed cooler already today.

"All righty, Beansy," she said to her dog. "You stay right there and take a nap. I'll be home in a little bit." The little pup looked at her like Amanda was abandoning her in her most dire need, but Amanda just laughed as she walked out.

She'd sobered by the time she pulled into the church parking lot. Finn waited for her on the bench outside the little building with the tall steeple, and she pulled in a breath at his presence. Yes, she had a serious crush on this man, and she felt herself falling all the way in love with him.

"Hey, there," she said as she approached.

He looked up from his phone, a smile blooming on that strong mouth. He kissed her as a way to say hello, and she linked her arm through his and took him toward the doors. She had been coming to this church for a very long time, and she knew almost all of the members who came as well.

She'd had several pastors over the years, but she'd always liked what they had to say. Perhaps she'd like the pastor in Dog Valley just as well. Finn didn't talk about the lessons much, but he went to church every week, so she knew his faith was strong and his commitment what Jason's could never be.

That had been enough for her. Until now, when she was thinking past the next date, or even the next month.

She wanted him at the Fall Festival with her. She wanted to see what he'd do for Halloween. She wanted him across the table from her at Thanksgiving, and she wanted to cuddle into him as the tree got lit at the lodge.

She was definitely thinking long-term with Finn, and that fact struck a bit of fear inside her heart even as she entered the most peaceful place she knew.

Beau had not left enough room for her and Finn on the end of the bench, and she detoured toward Andrew, who sat a few rows closer to the front on the side. "Is this okay?" she asked Finn, who looked a little bit like she'd just asked him to eat an entire rattlesnake.

"Fine," he said.

"Mom." Andrew stood up, his eyes flickering from her to Finn. "Sitting with us today?"

"Gramma," Chrissy said, wiggling in her mother's arms.

Amanda smiled at the girl and took her from Becca. "Can we?"

"Of course." Becca looked at Finn and stood up. "I'm Becca Whittaker. I haven't met you yet."

"Oh," Amanda said, glancing between them. "Andrew's wife. This is my boyfriend, Finn."

"You weren't at the Cupcake Wars?" he asked.

Becca smiled. "I wasn't feeling well." She slid down the bench, Andrew following her. "Andrew competed with Bree."

Amanda followed them onto the bench, settling Chrissy in her lap before Finn sat down beside her. Inside her purse, her phone started buzzing, but she ignored it as Chrissy held up two fingers.

"I two," she said to Finn, who chuckled.

"Yes, you are," Amanda said. "Now the preacher is getting up, so you have to be quiet."

"Sh." Chrissy put her chubby finger against her lips, the shushing louder than her normal voice.

Amanda giggled silently, looking at Finn to see a light in his eyes too. All at once, she realized he didn't have grandchildren yet. Incorporating her into his life would be a massive change, and she wondered if that was contributing to his unwillingness to ask her to give up her life here.

But her family wasn't included in what she'd have to give up.

Sitting in church with them will be, she thought, letting her granddaughter distract her from the pastor's message that day. Her mind had plenty to occupy it, and it just went around and around and around....

CHAPTER 16

Finn accepted the mug of hot apple cider Amanda gave him, the feeling in her house peaceful and beautiful. "Thank you," he said.

"So," she said, kicking off her heels and heading for the couch. "What did you think of church?"

"I liked it," he said. "Your pastor is...livelier than mine." She wouldn't like coming to church in Dog Valley, Finn knew that already. Still, he felt like he should ask her to come with him. So he did.

"Sure," she said. "Next week?"

"Whenever," he said, thinking about the chores he had to do that afternoon. He enjoyed spending time with Amanda, and she'd said they weren't at an impasse. Said she liked him, and he liked her a whole lot too.

He liked watching her with her grandchildren, and for the first time in his life, he wanted some of his own. He

LIZ ISAACSON

liked holding her hand, and he liked it when she said, "You're coming to the Fall Festival with me, right?"

"Right," he said.

"Have you been before?"

"Yeah," he said. "I got off the farm sometimes." He threw her a smile so she'd know he was teasing her.

She smiled, her light brown eyes practically glowing from within. When she looked at him like that, Finn thought everything between them would work out. He'd been hoping and praying for such a thing, as well as a good time to tell her more about his financial situation.

With a lull in the conversation, he felt like that time had arrived. "I have something to tell you," he said, clearing his throat and then taking a long sip of the cider. The liquid was way too hot for that, and he burned his tongue and the back of his mouth, all the way down his throat. He coughed, the pain making his eyes water.

"You can't slurp it," she said, leaning forward, concern in her eyes now.

Finn waved off her offer of ice water and set his cider down before he spilled it everywhere. "I'm okay," he said, but his throat still hurt. He met Amanda's eye and swallowed again.

"Remember how I said my last girlfriend cared more about my bank account than me?"

"Yes," she said.

"I, uh, have a lot of money."

She simply blinked at him. "Am I—I'm pretty sure I told you I did too."

150

"Yeah, I know." He started nodding, not sure why this point needed to be made so deliberately. But he felt like it did. "I don't *need* the farm," he said. "I haven't had to work for a while now."

Her eyebrows went up. "Oh?"

Finn looked away from her. "I was a software engineer for about a decade," he said. "I invented the software that encrypts logins, and it's the same type of thing that every major financial institution in the world uses today." He gave half a chuckle. "I've been a billionaire for over two decades. The farm is something I do because I love it."

Several long beats of silence passed. "And the gardening," she finally said. "You love that too."

He laughed lightly. "Yeah, I do." He didn't want to give up his farm, which meant that if they got married, he wanted her to leave her life here in Coral Canyon.

But he didn't *need* the farm in Dog Valley either. At least not to pay his bills. He hadn't said them together, but Amanda was smart. She'd hear the words anyway.

Finn did, and they boomed through him, making guilt rise within him over and over and over again.

"I'm going to be a judge for the pumpkin carving at the Fall Festival," she said, effectively changing the topic.

"That's great," he said, just adding her community involvement to the list of things he'd have to ask her to give up if he wanted her to be his permanently.

How in the world could he do that?

He didn't see any way that he ever could, and he wondered once again if they were simply from two different places—even if those places were only thirty minutes apart on a map.

THE WEEKS PASSED, and the weather grew colder. The pumpkins grew bigger. Amanda did drive to Dog Valley for church. Three times, in fact. She didn't like the pastor where Finn went to church, and he'd started attending with her every week in Coral Canyon.

Neither of them had brought up the next stage of their relationship. Finn hadn't, because he honesty had no idea what it was.

The weekend of the Fall Festival dawned with the threat of rain on the horizon. He'd already prepped the yard for the forthcoming winter, and he'd be surprised if that rain didn't turn to snow overnight.

Because of that, he packed a jacket in his truck and pulled a windbreaker over his long-sleeved shirt before he set out for Coral Canyon. He and Amanda were eating dinner at the park for their annual chili cookoff, and then she had to wander through the pumpkin patch to judge the carvings.

He'd be with her, of course, his hand steady in hers as she made her selections. Coral Canyon had a lot of activities during the day, but she'd said she'd be busy with her church group selling popcorn and soda and that he shouldn't come until evening.

That worked for him, because he could get the ranch

chores done early and be off until morning. So it was that he left the farm animals to govern themselves for the evening. Chocolate was already asleep when he walked out the front door, but Licorice followed him as if the black Lab would come with him.

"Stay here, bud," he said to the dog. "I'll be back." He seemed more antsy than usual, but Finn wasn't sure why.

He drove to Coral Canyon, and though his breath steamed in front of him as he hurried into the tent where dinner would be served, the weather had held off from dropping any precipitation.

Amanda's laugh drew him toward her, and he couldn't help the irregular way his heart thumped in his chest. She was lovely, with such happiness shining on her face. She turned toward him as if his presence called to her, and she excused herself from the group of people she spoke with.

She practically skipped toward him, and Finn felt her joy infuse right into his soul. In that moment, he knew he was in love with this woman, and there was absolutely nothing he could do about it now.

"Hey, stranger," she said, grasping his biceps as she pressed into him and kissed him. "You have got to try these maple doughnuts I made this afternoon."

Surprise darted through Finn. "I thought you were here all afternoon."

"Oh, I was." She beamed at him, securing her hand in his. "But I got dragged into the baking competition when Millie came down with something. She already had the spot, and I took it." She tugged on his hand to get him moving with her. "I think I could win. I mean, they're just doughnuts, but they're pretty good."

"I'm sure they are," he said, allowing the happiness of this day, this moment with her, to move through him powerfully.

She led him over to the baked goods that had come from the competition earlier in the day, and she paused in front of the table. "There's only a couple left," she said. "Better grab one."

Finn did, stepping past her and willing to knock someone to the ground if he had to. After all, he'd sampled Amanda's baking before, and it was worthy of throwing an elbow. In the end, he didn't have to get physical to get a doughnut, and the sugary, maple glaze burst against his taste buds in such a way that made him smile immensely.

"Good, right?" she asked, as if she needed validation.

"So good," he said, popping the last bite of pastry into his mouth. "Who needs chili now?"

She giggled, latched onto his arm, and steered him toward the group of people she'd been chatting with earlier. "Everyone," she said. "This is Finn Barber."

"Hello, Finn," several people said. More choruses of hellos met his ears, and he smiled at the vibrancy of this older group of people. Comprised of men and women, he recognized them all from the congregation on Sundays.

"Do you have snow in Dog Valley?" Lois asked. Finn had met her a few times over the last several weeks, as she was Amanda's best friend and lived just down the lane from her. Apparently the two helped each other with canning and other household projects from time to time.

"Not yet," he said. "I wouldn't be surprised if it snows tonight."

"Hold your tongue," she said with a smile. "I'm not ready for that."

"Me either," Amanda said. "I really don't like winter."

Finn had heard her say that before, and yet, she'd stayed in Wyoming after Ron had died. Of course, most of her sons were here, and apparently, several years ago, they'd all been here.

Finn had yet to meet Eli, but he'd heard plenty about Amanda's second son. He didn't know what else to say to add to the conversation, and thankfully, a microphone crackled to life a man said, "It's time for the chili dinner. You must have a pink ticket to attend this event, and we'll be taking those near the west doors."

Finn wasn't worried though he didn't have a pink ticket. Amanda would have one for him, as she was the one who was well-connected in Coral Canyon. Sure enough, she handed the two tickets to the man taking them near the set of doors where Finn had entered the tent.

The atmosphere was everything he'd expect from a small-town celebration, with laughter and good conversation, and even better food. The chili had been provided by several churches across the town of Coral Canyon, and it seemed like the loaves and fishes and never ran out.

Patrons had brought cornbread and salads to go with

the chili, and Finn found a particularly delicious "salad" made mostly of cookies, whipped cream, and apples.

Several people said hello to Amanda, and he saw her in a whole new light. She was a pillar of this community, and he wasn't sure how he could ever take her from that house where all her memories lived, from her beloved congregation, or from this town who loved her and whom she clearly loved too.

She'd said nothing about it, though, and he decided to take things one day at a time. At this moment, it was one hour before Amanda said, "Come on, dear. You promised you'd brave the cold to help me judge the pumpkin carving."

He knew his opinion would have no sway over the winners, but he wanted to be where she was, so he went with her, flipping up the collar on his windbreaker as he stepped out into the darkening sky.

CHAPTER 17

A manda couldn't seem to feel the chill in the air though it was definitely there. Finn's hand in hers felt so solid and so right, and the flickering faces of the pumpkins brought happiness to her whole soul.

"Autumn is my favorite season," she said to Finn, her voice too loud outside the tent, where everything echoed. There were considerably less people out here too, and the sky seemed to swallow her words whole.

"Really?" Finn asked. "I would've guessed spring or summer. I know it's not winter."

"I don't understand how anyone's favorite season can be winter."

"Well, there's no yard work to be done. The farm chores aren't as intense. Plenty of time to soak up the sun with the pine trees."

Amanda let his words roll through her. "Pine tree love.

I didn't know that about you." And she knew a lot about this gentle man beside her. Wanted to know everything.

"Glad I can still surprise you," he said. They passed under the arch leading to Jack O'Lantern Lane, and Amanda pulled out the tiny notebook she'd brought with her. She was supposed to vote for her ten favorites sometime before nine p.m.

She'd been at the park all day long, and she was honestly ready to go home. Make sure Beans had enough food and water, maybe make some hot broth, and crawl into bed. Her bones felt old and weary, and while she did love autumn, she didn't like the way the temperature affected her.

"These are so creative," she said as they walked oh-so-slowly. Most of the pumpkins didn't simply have a face. The carving here was serious, with scenes shining through from the light within the gourds. The loop around was half a mile, and she felt a responsibility to look at all of them, even once she had her ten choices.

Every so often, she'd erased one number off and put a new one on in its place. Eventually, after what felt like a very long time, she had her final list.

She dropped it in the box just inside the arch and turned to Finn. "I'm ready to go now."

"Already?"

"Yes." She pressed into him and touched her lips to his. "Take me home, cowboy?"

"Mm." He kissed her properly, swiping that cowboy hat from his head. "Ready when you are."

With a satisfied smile, she laced her hand through his and started for the parking lot. She didn't want to admit it, but she felt stuck with Finn, the same way she'd been with Jason for so long.

He'd said he wasn't ready to ask her to leave her life in Coral Canyon, but that had been a while ago now. Would he ever be ready for her to do that?

Ever since he'd said he didn't need the farm to pay his bills, she'd been wondering if he'd ever leave Dog Valley and come to her house to make their life together. But every time she thought about it, she knew he wouldn't.

She didn't even want him there. That had been her and Ron's house, and it still felt like it to her. It would be much easier to move to Dog Valley and take up residence in Finn's house. But she didn't want to go to church there, and she simply couldn't see herself missing the Coral Canyon festivities she loved so much.

Finn followed her as she turned onto her lane, and Amanda immediately knew something was wrong at her house. A truck sat in the circle drive, and a light shone out the front window when she hadn't left that lamp on.

"Jason," she said to herself as she parked behind his truck instead of pulling into her driveway. Anxiety hit her hard. She hadn't spoken to him in months; what in the world was he doing here?

She got out of her SUV and approached Finn's truck. "My ex-boyfriend is here," she said, nodding toward the front of the house as the door opened and the man she'd been with for so long appeared.

Finn looked that direction and back at her. "Want me to come in? Or do you need to handle something on your own?"

Amanda honestly didn't know. She hadn't dwelt on Jason much, at least not with Finn. "I better go see what he's doing here alone." She'd taken one step when Finn put his hand on her arm.

"Why didn't you take the next step with him?"

She'd wanted to, but she couldn't tell Finn that now. Could she? It hadn't mattered before. He knew she'd dated a lot more than him. That had apparently satisfied him.

"We didn't share the same values," she said. "I stayed with him for a long time, hoping." His hand fell away, and she walked down the front sidewalk toward the porch. As she climbed the steps, she asked, "What are you doing here, Jason?"

"I still have your keys," he said, holding them out to her.

"How long have you been here?" She took the keys, the solid, sharp feel of them in her hand comforting somehow.

"How long have you two been dating?" He nodded to where Finn still stood beside his truck. He watched them, not even trying to hide it.

"A few months," Amanda said, sure Jason was here about something more than keys. "Why didn't you call before coming?"

"I did," he said, finally taking his eyes from Finn. "Three times. You wouldn't pick up."

"I didn't get any calls from you," she said.

"Did you get a new phone?"

"No."

"Then I called."

Amanda didn't like the bite in his tone, and she wanted him to leave. He was still as handsome as ever, and she reminded herself that they really didn't have the same values. Their relationship would never work, even if she wanted it to.

With a jolt, she wondered if she was doing the same thing with Finn. Could she be happy on that farm, thirty minutes from everything she'd known for almost five decades?

"How long have you been here?" she asked again.

"I don't know who he is," Jason said, turning toward her. "I don't care." He reached for her hands and took them in his. "I want to try again with you."

Amanda looked up into his dark eyes—eyes she'd loved so much once. She shook her head. "It's too late for that, Jason."

"Why?"

She didn't know. Only that it was. He'd hurt her too much with his refusals to forgive, and she was happy with Finn.

"I think I'm in love with him," she said, facing Finn.

"You loved me once," Jason said, stepping behind her and running his hand along her waist. He knew how to make her feel young and sexy, and Amanda almost fell for his charms again. But she knew he hadn't changed.

"Sorry, Jason," she said, stepping away from his touch. "You should go." She walked to the door and opened it. "Thanks for bringing my keys back." She slipped inside, feeling cowardly and weak by leaving Finn out there to face Jason alone.

Her phone chimed, and she saw Finn's message flash across the top of her screen. *Open your garage.*

She bustled through the house to get the garage open, and Finn pulled in where she usually parked. He hit the button as he climbed the few steps and took her in his arms.

"Did you know it's very quiet out here?" he whispered. "And I could hear your whole conversation?"

Amanda's heart tapped around inside her chest, first from the way he held her so tightly against him. And second, because he'd heard her say she thought she was in love with him.

"Is that true?" he asked. "You're in love with me?"

"I said I *thought* I was," she whispered. Her voice had apparently decided to go on a hiatus.

"I *know* I'm in love with you," he murmured, his mouth touching hers. He teased and brushed his lips along hers before fully claiming them. And Amanda knew then that she was in love with him too.

"I'M GOING to move to Dog Valley," she told Lois a few days later. She hadn't told a single other person. Finn had not proposed, though he had stayed too late, and she kissed him for too long standing right there in the mudroom off the garage. He'd not said anything else about it, but if they loved each other, they couldn't keep living thirty minutes apart. She'd learned that when she was eighteen years old.

"You are?" Lois looked up from the pot of applesauce she was stirring. "When? Why?"

"My boyfriend lives there," Amanda said. *And he loves me.* Warmth moved through her, and she couldn't help smiling, though she aimed it at the rings she was making to put in the oven. Lois's grandchildren loved dried apple rings. Amanda did too.

"You're going to leave Coral Canyon?" Lois asked again.

"Why is this so shocking?"

"I just didn't think you would," she said. "Even after Ron died, you stayed in that house. I just don't see how you can go now."

"It's just a house," Amanda said, but she knew it wasn't. It was *her* house. The house where she and Ron had built their entire lives. If she thought about it for too long, she grew nostalgic and sad.

"Just a house." Lois scoffed. "You had Beau in that house. It's *not* just a house."

Amanda didn't say anything else. She didn't have to defend herself. As she continued to help Lois put up the jars of applesauce she wanted, she couldn't help thinking of the years of her life she'd spent raising her boys.

They were good times. But that didn't mean she had to stay in them. Her sons rarely came to her house anymore, and perhaps it was simply time to let it go.

Amanda wasn't great at doing that, but she had to get better. If she let go of the house, would she finally be able to let go of Ron too?

With a sudden start that left her breathless, she realized she was as much to blame for her and Jason's failed relationship as he was. She hadn't been able to commit to him.

Could she commit to Finn? Or was she still fooling herself into thinking she was ready for a new life companion?

CHAPTER 18

Finn pulled his jacket tighter around himself and zipped it up. The sky looked like the devil himself had whipped up a storm to unleash on the Teton Mountain valley, but he had animals to feed. Hay to move. Chickens to take care of, so they didn't freeze.

He thought he might freeze to death before he even stepped off his deck, what with the wind whipping around like it was.

Frowning at the sky, he hurried down the steps and across the backyard, mentally moving through his checklist.

It had snowed a few weeks ago, just after the Fall Festival in Coral Canyon, but that had melted pretty quickly. The kids had gotten in their trick-or-treating last week, but Finn felt sure the snow would come again tonight—and stay.

He wasn't quite ready for winter to set in again,

despite all the things about it he did like. His breath steamed in front of him as he walked toward the stables, trying to decide if he could put off a couple of the stalls he had slated to be cleaned today.

One step through the doors, and he knew he couldn't. It smelled bad in there, and he hurried down the row of horses to find Gone With the Wind lying down.

"Hey," he said to the mare. "Are you okay?"

She clearly wasn't okay. The horse had been sick, and the stall needed to be cleaned. She needed a bath, and several more tasks got added to Finn's list—including airing out the barn.

It hadn't started to snow yet, so he opened all the doors leading out to the corral and let the other horses get outside for a bit. Gone With the Wind stood up, and Finn let her go too, though he'd be bringing her back in soon enough.

He put on gloves and made quick work of cleaning out the stalls on his list for the day. He hosed down Wind's and added fresh straw to it. Then he moved down to the washing stalls and got the water going before bringing her back inside.

She was a stubborn thing, and she didn't enjoy getting bathed. He collected a quick sample of muck from her coat before leading her into the spray. Hopefully, she'd recover quickly, but he'd take that to the vet on his way to Coral Canyon that afternoon.

He and Amanda had tickets to a play at the community theater there. Apparently, one of the girls in her church congregation had landed one of the leading roles, and Amanda wanted to support her.

"Come on, Windy," he said, tugging on the reins to get the horse to move. She glared at him, and he glared right back. "You're covered in sick," he reasoned. "The water is warm."

Apparently, she didn't care about warm water, and Finn ended up as wet as she was by the time he got her cleaned up. Frustrated, and with miles of chores to go, he pulled out his phone and texted Amanda that he might have to meet her at the theater.

Everything okay? she sent back.

Just a sick horse. And he had to shower again now, too. He fed all the thoroughbreds, closed all the outside doors, and locked everything up tight. "All right, guys," he said to the equines he loved so much. "I have to go. I'll come check on you tonight."

He'd be getting home late, which was fine. He'd still come out in the dark and make sure they all had the water and feed they needed. That Windy wasn't sick again.

As he hurried over to the hay barn, he called the vet and said, "Hey, Wilson. It's Finn."

"What's goin' on, Finn?" he asked, and Finn realized it was Saturday.

"You're not in today, are you?"

"Not usually."

"I'm sorry," Finn said. "I just have a horse that was lying down this morning. Been sick overnight."

"Got a sample?"

LIZ ISAACSON

"Yes."

"Bring it by. I'll look at it," he said. "I'm at home."

"Thanks, Wilson," he said.

"See you soon."

Finn ducked into the henhouse to check on the heat lamps. They seemed to be working fine, and he tossed some seed on the ground and checked water troughs before heading to the hay barn.

He worked, and worked, and worked to get everything done on the farm in anticipation of being gone for several hours with snow on the way. His dogs trotted around with him everywhere he went, until Chocolate made a mad dash for the fence, barking his fool head off.

"Chocolate," Finn said, his head pounding. "Enough." He didn't need the noise on top of the stress. Anxiety and frustration mingled together, especially when the chocolate Lab didn't stop and return to him.

Finn focused beyond the dog, out into the fields where he stood. His tail wagged and wagged, as if a friend was coming to see him, but what Finn saw wasn't a welcome guest.

"A moose," he said as the majestic animal moved closer. He looked like he was loping along, barely moving, and Finn was struck with wonder. He loved wildlife, had a deep respect for it.

But he also knew moose were particularly moody and could cause a great deal of damage to dogs, humans, and anything else that got in their path.

"Come on," he said, whistling to get Chocolate away

168

from the fence. "Let's go, guys." He started for the house, ready to get out of the wind, out of the cold, and into the hot shower.

He kept his eyes on the moose for several steps backward, but it had stopped. "Chocolate," Finn barked, and the dog finally turned and trotted toward him.

"Good boy," he said, twisting and walking forward now. "Let's get inside." Relief filled him as he climbed the steps to the deck and held the door open for his canines.

Once everyone was safely inside, Finn peered through the window to find the moose had disappeared. He had high fences to keep the deer and moose off his property, as he didn't spend hours in his yard pruning and tending to his roses to have them all eaten for breakfast. He didn't think the moose had wandered onto his property, but he didn't want to lose a goat or a chicken to the wild animal. He didn't want to hit it with his truck, that was for sure.

He showered and got on the road toward Coral Canyon in time to pick up Amanda. He texted her, but she didn't respond.

He went to her house anyway, hoping she'd received his message and would be ready. The snow started to fall as he pulled into her circle drive, and he dashed through the white stuff to ring the doorbell.

She didn't come, and Finn suddenly just wanted to go home. Get some dinner and sit on his couch, something playing on the TV in front of him. He still hadn't eaten, and he hoped the theater had concessions of some kind.

But Amanda wouldn't come to the door.

He pulled out his phone and called her, turning toward his truck as if he might hurry back to it and get over to the theater. She obviously wasn't here.

Her phone rang, and he tilted his head as he heard it in two places. One through his phone and one inside her house.

So she had to be here.

He hung up and tried the doorknob. "Amanda?" he called, scanning the house the way he had the stables earlier that day.

He didn't notice anything out of the ordinary. But there was definitely something not right here. She wasn't in the study off the foyer, nor the living room, dining room, or kitchen. Her phone sat on the kitchen counter, and surely she wouldn't have left it to go out in this weather.

He stepped through the mudroom and checked the garage. Her car was here. She *had* to be here.

"Amanda?" he called again, louder this time. Maybe she'd fallen and been hurt. Couldn't get to her phone. His pulse accelerated, and he turned his attention to the steps. Could she be upstairs? Her bedroom was on the main floor, and he knew she didn't use those upstairs bedrooms very often.

So he detoured over to the hallway that led deeper into the house, and the distinct sound of someone crying met his ears.

"Amanda?" he asked softly, pushing open her ajar bedroom door.

She sat on the floor, dozens of photo albums spread

before her. She still hadn't heard him or acknowledged him, and he heard her murmur, "I'm so sorry, Ron. I miss you so much."

His heartbeat pumped ice cold blood into his veins, and he froze. What was she sorry about?

Of course he knew she'd always love her husband, but it sounded like she wasn't ready for another committed relationship.

Foolishness hit him with the force of a blizzard, and he felt blinded. He hadn't expected that at all, and he probably should have. No matter what, he could never ask her to leave this house. Leave her support system. Her church. Her friends.

He turned to leave, his foot kicking the doorjamb and drawing her attention.

"Finn," she said, her voice full of surprise.

"I'm sorry," he said automatically. "I knocked. I called you. When you didn't come...." He trailed off, not sure how to finish. "What is all this?"

"Just memories," she said, swiping at her eyes and turning away from him to stand up. She faced him, apprehension on her face now.

Finn searched and searched her face, trying to find an answer he didn't know existed. "Amanda, I'm not feeling up to the play."

That much was true.

"I'm not either, truth be told," she said.

He took in the vast amount of memories spread out on her bedroom floor. There were a couple of baby outfits and shoes, as well as some framed items he couldn't see very well from where he stood in the doorway.

"How long have you been in here, looking at this stuff?" he asked.

"I don't know." She sighed and ran her hands up and down her arms. "I need to turn on the furnace. It's cold in here."

It was cold in there, and Finn felt the chill all the way into his bones. "Amanda," he said. "Do we—I mean, I feel like we need to talk about this."

"What?" she asked, though she had to know.

"Your memories." He indicated the spread on the floor. "I don't see how you're ever going to leave this house."

Fresh tears gathered in her eyes, and she pressed her lips tightly together. "I can't disagree."

Finn felt like someone had slapped the air out of his lungs. "I—" He didn't know what else to say. She'd just said so much with only three words.

Three words.

He knew the power of three other words, and he did love Amanda. He'd told her in more than three words, but he'd said it nonetheless. He couldn't take it back now, though everything inside him wanted to.

"I need to go," he said.

"Finn," she said, her voice breaking. The tears tracked down her cheeks. "I'm just—"

"Not ready," he said. "I understand." But he didn't. He also didn't want to be a jerk. He hadn't lost his wife, and he honestly had no idea what she was going through.

She stepped over to him and put her hand on his arm. "I don't want to break up."

"But you don't want to be with me where I am," he said. "What else is there to do?" He thought of her previous boyfriend, the man who'd been on her porch after the Fall Festival. "Is this why you and Jason didn't work out?"

Something flashed through her eyes even as she shook her head. "No."

Finn wanted to stay. He wanted to go. The war raged inside him, and he finally said, "Amanda, I need to go."

Her hand fell from his arm as he backed up. He turned and walked away, and she let him go. It was the worst feeling in the world, and Finn hated every step he took away from her.

But she didn't call him back, and that felt like a break-up to him.

CHAPTER 19

A manda added more salt to the pumpkin soup, her remedy to a terrible, awful, no-good snow day.

She'd put away all of the photo albums. All the mementos from her sons' childhoods. All the pieces of jewelry Ron had bought her over the years. She could put away the physical things, but she couldn't rid herself of the memories.

She could hear his laughter in the walls, see her boys as they wrestled on the couches in the living room, relive the dinners they used to share in the evenings.

She hated that Finn had found her crying over old things. She'd been planning to just look for a few minutes, but hours had slipped by. As the snow fell last night after Finn had left, she'd continued to look through the good times of her life, remembering all the fun she'd had as a young mother. All the joy she'd seen in her sons. All the hard times when Ron worked too late. The times when the kids were sick.

Through all of that, she'd realized Finn was right. She didn't want to be with him where he was. She wanted him to come here, to this house, so she could make new memories there—with him.

She felt so stupid. So selfish. Because of that, she hadn't been able to call him last night or this morning. She'd spent the first few hours after waking up baking a chocolate cherry cake for Brianna, who they were supposed to see in the play the previous evening.

She'd spent a few minutes at the younger woman's home, the cake a gift and an apology at the same time. Now, after church, which she'd attended alone, she bent over her recipe book, wondering how much curry was too much. In her opinion, such a thing couldn't happen, and she was probably going to be the only one who'd eat this soup.

So she heaved in another palm full of the spice and stirred it into the simmering broth before adding the shredded chicken and wild rice.

Her phone chimed, and she practically jumped out of her skin with the sound. It was Eli, and a smile immediately formed on her face.

Coming for Thanksgiving!

He'd had to put a few things in order at the resort he managed before he could fully commit, and he must've done so.

That's great news, she sent back to him, her fingers a bit sticky against her screen. As she washed her hands, she realized Eli and his family would stay at the lodge. She hurried to pick up her phone again and ask him *Will you consider staying here? I'd love to have guests.*

While she was at it, she texted all her sons in the family text and said, *I want to host Thanksgiving dinner at my house this year. What do you all think?*

She sent the message, and then added, *I'll talk to Celia. I know she's very much a part of our family. And the Everett's, and Bree and Annie, and anyone else who wants to come. We'll just do it here instead of at the lodge. There's plenty of space.*

And there was.

She and Ron had specifically built this house to be able to host everyone who ever wanted to come through the door. And she wanted them here this year. It would be the first time since Ron had died, and it was time.

Sure, Beau said.

Of course, Graham texted.

We'll stay with you, Mom, Eli said.

Only Andrew didn't answer right away, but Chrissy had been sick that day, and Becca wasn't feeling well either. He was probably attending to his family, and he'd respond when he finally got back to his phone.

Is this you wanting to show off your culinary skills for Finn? Beau asked, a wink following the question.

Amanda almost scoffed, but the sound morphed into a sob right there in her throat.

Finn.

How could she go through the holidays without him?

She'd been so excited to share the Christmas traditions at the lodge with him, and now she wouldn't be able to.

We broke up. She stared at the words before sending them zipping to all of her son's devices.

Not surprisingly, Graham called ten seconds later. "Mom," he said. "What happened?"

"I don't know," Amanda said, though she knew perfectly well. She just didn't want to admit that it was her fault. Her throat tightened, and she couldn't say anything else.

"I thought you guys were getting along so great," he said as another call beeped in her ear.

"Beau's calling," she said.

"Of course he is," Graham said. "He can wait. Mom."

She didn't like the way he said *Mom*, but she did appreciate the concern she heard in his voice. "Graham, I—I'm not sure I'm ready to get remarried."

"Really?" he asked. "You've been dating for years. Finn's not the first guy you've been out with. Heck, you dated Jason forever."

"Yeah," she said. Dated. There was no commitment there, and she knew it.

"What happened?" Graham asked. "I thought he was a great fit for you."

"He was," she said. "He is."

"I'm so confused," Graham said.

Amanda took a deep breath and blew it out. "It's not that confusing, Graham. He lives in Dog Valley. I live here."

"He can't move?"

"He has a very successful farm there, and he's not ready to give it up."

"Then why can't you—?"

"Beau's calling again," she said. "I'm going to switch over. I'll talk to you later, Graham."

"I can set you up with someone else," he yelled into the phone, but Amanda ended the call without answering him.

No, thank you. She would not be going on another blind date. She didn't want to date anyone, period.

Because you're in love with Finn Barber.

"Hello, Beau," she said, wishing she'd said nothing. She'd known her sons would call, and she'd have to explain things she didn't fully understand herself.

"Mom," he said, his voice filled with compassion. "Why did you break up with Finn?"

"Actually," she said, a fresh wave of agony rolling through her. "He broke up with me."

AMANDA PULLED the pecan pie from the oven as the sun lit Thanksgiving Day. Eli and Meg and their kids had arrived yesterday afternoon, and she'd enjoyed having their laughter and presence in her house so much.

She'd finished a couple of chocolate pies while her grandson, Stockton, told her all about his surfing lessons in California. She'd chopped up the bread cubes for the stuffing and left them out to dry.

A soft knock sounded on the front door, and she hurried toward it to let Celia in. "Morning," she said, getting blasted with the chill of the day. There had been snow on the ground for weeks now, and Amanda still didn't know how to enjoy it the way Finn had suggested.

Frustration pulled through her as she hugged Celia, because Finn still seemed to be stuck in the center of her mind.

She took the bowls Celia carried and stepped back so the other woman could come into the house. "Come in, come in. It's freezing out there."

"Did Eli make it in okay last night?" Celia asked. "I heard they closed the road between here and Jackson."

"They did," she said. "But he flew in early and made it before the worst of the storm hit." She hoped Finn would be able to get to see his daughters. She tried to push the thought away. She didn't even know what Finn's plans were for the holiday. They'd broken up nine-teen days ago, and she hadn't yet invited him to any Thanksgiving or Christmas festivities with her or her family.

But she assumed he'd go see Joann and Kimberly. Or have them out to the farm. But with the roads closed, he might be alone today.

Her heart bled, and she seriously considered calling him. No one should be alone on Thanksgiving.... She hesi-tated, and Celia tied an apron around her waist and said,

"Those pies look delicious," snapping Amanda out of her mind.

"I'm putting the turkey in now," she said, setting the bowls on the counter for Celia. "You're doing the stuffing, yes? I have the bread there, and everything you asked for is in the fridge or on the counter."

"Stuffing," Celia confirmed. They began working together in the kitchen, and Amanda's heart started to fill and fill. This was what she wanted. Her house filled with love and laughter. Friends and family. The scent of sage and butter, browning bread and hot pumpkin pie.

They chatted easily about happenings around town, including the announcement of a new shopping mall coming to town.

"Coral Canyon is growing so much," Celia said.

"I actually like it," Amanda said. "We're getting good restaurants, and I love having more options for shopping."

"You know what?" Celia asked with a smile. "So do I."

"How's your daughter?" Amanda asked, but before Celia could answer, a little boy yelled and footsteps pounded down the steps.

Amanda laughed and went to greet Stockton, who had Averie following him as quickly as her little legs could carry her. "Guys," she said. "Who wants breakfast?" She didn't see Meg or Eli, and she hoped they'd take the chance to sleep in a little. "I have some of that chocolate cereal you like, Stocky."

He cheered, and Amanda's heart warmed as he helped Averie up onto the barstool. Amanda got out two bowls and fed her grandchildren before getting back to work peeling potatoes. Lunch wasn't for another few hours, but it took a colossal amount of work to get every dish done at the same time for the number of people who'd be eating with her that day.

The time wore on, and Eli finally appeared to take the children upstairs to shower and get ready for the day.

Graham and his family arrived, followed closely by Beau and Andrew, their wives and children. Amanda couldn't stop smiling, and tears kept springing to the back of her eyes at the strangest of times.

She couldn't shake Finn from her mind, though no one asked about him. He probably wouldn't even be able to drive here, if the roads were really that bad.

Vi and Todd arrived, saying the snow had finally stopped and the sun was shining. Rose, Liam, and Jack and Fran Everett came bearing freshly baked rolls. Amanda took them and put them on the counter before giving hugs around to everyone. Then she quickly ducked into the mudroom and tapped out a text to Finn.

Are you alone today? You're welcome at my house for Thanksgiving dinner. We're eating in about an hour.

She stared at the letters, making sure they were all right. Her heart thumped in her chest. She wasn't sure if she should send this message. Would he find her overbearing? Maddening? Would he simply be annoyed by it?

Amanda thought she probably would be, and there was no way she'd ever drive to his house for a holiday party simply because she was alone. As if she was an afterthought.

So she quickly erased the text and looked up from her phone. Taking a deep breath, she stared at the wall across from her.

"Mom?" Graham called, and she sniffed, holding back her tears.

"Yeah," she said as she stepped out of the mudroom. "I'm here."

"Celia says there's no more butter."

"I bought tons of butter," Amanda said, returning to the kitchen. Graham stepped in front of her.

"Hey, are you okay?" He put his arm around her.

Amanda leaned into him, stealing a bit of strength from her older son. He was the same height and build as her husband, and so many memories and feelings surged to the surface. "Yes," she said, her voice breaking. "I just…I'm so happy everyone's here."

She stepped back and wiped her face. "I'm okay. I am."

"All right," he said, stepping out of the way. "Better go solve that butter emergency."

CHAPTER 20

F inn kept the news on as he put the finishing touches on the dips he'd been asked to bring to Thanksgiving dinner. Kim had called last night to say the roads had been closed, and they could postpone their noon start time to four o'clock.

Jackson Hole sat an hour and a half away, and he needed to leave soon in order to make it on time. He knew he could make it to Coral Canyon, and the road between there and Jackson was usually plowed first.

So he listened, hoping he'd be able to make it to the celebration at his daughter's house. He enjoyed the silence inside his own home too, but he didn't want to give thanks alone. Not today. Not after the last few weeks where he'd had his fill of silence, of being alone, of wondering why he'd thought opening himself up to a relationship was a good idea.

He finally learned that the roads were open, but four-wheel-drive and chains were recommended. Another storm was expected overnight, and Finn loaded up his dips and boxes of crackers and headed out.

Along the way, he called a hotel he'd stayed at several times in Jackson Hole and booked a room for that night. As soon as that was finished, he called Zach, his best friend in Dog Valley. They worked together in the spring to get their farms back in shape after a long winter.

"Are you in town?" he asked, as Zach had as much money as him and traveled sometimes.

"Yeah," Zach said. "Need help in all the snow?"

"Yes," Finn said, squinting as the sun made an appearance and started glinting off all the fresh snowfall. "I'm headed to my daughter's house in Jackson right now. I'm going to stay the night. Wondering if you can get over to the farm tonight and check on everyone. Let the dogs out. Go back in the morning. Or you can just stay at my place."

"Sure," Zach said. "I'll take care of it."

"Thanks," Finn said, relief filling him. "I'll be back by noon, I would think. I'll let you know if I'm not." With another storm coming in, he had no idea what the weather or road conditions would be like in the morning.

"Sounds good," Zach said.

"Thanks." Finn hung up, glad he had a few things taken care of. He didn't want to admit it, but he was also glad he could think about something besides the farm for the next twenty-four hours.

He absolutely loved his farm, and normally he didn't mind the work the animals and land required. But it would be nice to go on vacation every once in a while and not have to make special arrangements, worry that his diva horses wouldn't eat, or that a chicken would freeze to death because the heat lamps had to be adjusted just-so.

With the radio on loud, he continued toward Jackson Hole, ready to see his daughters and be with people.

The last few weeks without Amanda had been extremely difficult, and Finn had cut himself off from others completely. He hadn't been to church, and he'd been relying on the grocery delivery service so he didn't even have to go shopping.

It wasn't healthy, and he didn't like how he felt. But he didn't know what to do about it.

"You sure know how to pick 'em," he muttered to himself, knowing he wasn't being entirely fair. Maybe with Tiffany, who had only wanted to inherit his money. But how was he to know Amanda wasn't truly ready to move on?

She'd been dating for years, which was more than he'd done. She'd seemed ready, and he once again considered selling his farm. He could sell the horses to other breeders, pack up everything he owned, and show up on her doorstep. He'd beg her to take him back, and tell her he'd live wherever she wanted, as long as they were together.

But he was too proud to do such a thing.

At least the long drive passed quickly with thoughts of Amanda in his mind. Kim dashed out to help him bring in the food he'd brought, all smiles and hellos. His spirits lifted at the sight of family, at the warmth that spilled from the front door as he went inside her house.

"Dad," she said just inside the door. "My boyfriend is here."

"No ring yet?" Finn whispered, glancing around.

"Not yet, Dad." She nodded toward a dark-haired man standing in the kitchen with another man Finn didn't know. "Everyone," she called in a loud voice. "My dad is here." She stepped toward the kitchen with the armful of crackers, a wide smile on her face. "His name's Finn, and he's the best horse trainer in the world."

Smiling faces turned toward him, and he lifted his hand in a general hello. Kim had invited anyone from her church group that didn't have somewhere else to go, and seven people had gathered besides Kim, Joann, and Kim's boyfriend.

She linked her arm through his and guided him over to Finn, who set down the two bowls of dips he'd prepared. "Dad," she said. "This is Josiah Crawley. Jos, my dad."

"It's great to meet you, sir," Jos said, extending his hand for Finn to shake.

He had a good air about him, and Finn smiled at him. "I've heard a lot about you." He shook the man's hand. "Own a deli, is that right?"

"Yes, sir."

"You don't have to call him sir," Kim said with a laugh.

"You really don't," Finn said. "Makes me feel old, like my dad."

"You *are* old, Dad," Kim teased.

Finn chuckled as he lifted his cowboy hat and ran his hand through his hair. "I suppose I'm grayer than I used to be."

"You should see Mom," Joann said, stepping over to the group. "And she refuses to cover it up."

"I think she looks good," Kim said.

"What's she doing for the holiday?" Finn asked. "Something with Heath's parents?"

"Yes, they're going on a church-service mission in January, so they're trying to spend as much time with them as possible." Joann handed him a tall glass of sparkling cider. "It's apple-grape, Daddy."

"Thanks, princess." He took a sip, glad to be here and not alone.

"See Clara over there?" Joann edged around him until she was nearly behind him. "She's only a couple of years younger than you. Now that you and Amanda aren't—"

"No," Finn said, a little harsher than he meant to.

"Dad, you deserve someone great."

Amanda was great, and he didn't want anyone else. He hadn't mentioned that to Joann or Kim, and he'd let them assume that she had turned out to be like Tiffany. Kim had suggested it, and Finn hadn't argued.

"Dad—" Joanna started, her eyes wide and earnest.

"Girls," he said. "I need to tell you something." He closed their little circle and glanced at Jos as he cleared his throat. "I broke up with Amanda. Not the other way around. And she has more money than I do, so it wasn't because of that."

Joann's mouth gaped, and Kim gasped. "Dad. Why? You liked her so much."

"I know," he said. "But our lives…it's really hard to merge lives and memories and families when you're as old as we are." He shook his head, an overwhelming sadness descending on him. "It just didn't work out. She…she'd have to give up too much to be with me, and she didn't want to do it."

Joann hugged him tight, and Finn welcomed the action. "So she broke up with you, then."

"No." He stepped back, his stomach grumbling. "I ended it with her so she wouldn't have to choose. After all, no one wants to come in second to a house." And she hadn't done that, but he still knew what Amanda would've picked.

And that knowledge burned more than anything.

⚜

HE MADE it back to his farm the next day without issue. Another day bled into another night, and then a new morning. November faded to December, and his daughters would be spending the Christmas holidays with their mother.

Finn returned to church, hoping there would be someone willing to take in strays like Kim had done in Jackson Hole for Thanksgiving. He often attended a function like that, taking the Goodman sisters with him. With only a couple of weeks left, he hadn't heard of anything this year.

His other option was to return to Kentucky and visit his parents. They were getting older, but his mother had assured him that his father was just as stubborn and just as invested in his horses.

He knew if he called his mother and asked if he could come, she'd probably faint. Then she'd pick herself up and buy his plane ticket for him. She'd invited him to come visit dozens of times, and he hadn't been home in twenty years. Not since he'd retired from the software industry, his billions already in the bank, and started his farm here in Dog Valley.

The phone rang, and then his mother said, "Finn, it's good to hear from you."

"Hello, Mother," he said.

"How are the horses?"

"Fine, fine," he said, suddenly thinking he'd owe Zach something huge to get him to come take care of the farm if he flew to Kentucky and Barber Farms. He wasn't sure he could make that drive down those lanes with the blindingly white fences.

At the same time, it was definitely time to do so.

"What are your plans for the holidays?" he asked.

"Rhonda and Jones are coming," she said. "But the week after. They're going to their daughter's for the actual holiday to watch darling Jasmine open her gifts."

Finn would like to see his sister again, so he said, "I'd like to come while they're there."

Silence came through the line. "Is this Finn?" his mother finally asked.

Finn chuckled, though he knew he'd removed himself from his family. He was on speaking terms with his sister, his mother, and even his father. He knew about his nieces and nephews, as well as their children.

He just didn't go to much. Anything. He didn't go to anything.

"They're coming the twenty-seventh," she said. "There's plenty of room for you here. It's still just you?"

He knew she didn't mean for the words to cut him, but they did. Sliced right down to the bone and kept going.

"Yes," he managed to say. "Still just me." He was suddenly grateful he'd never told his mother about Amanda, and as he hung up, he realized he still didn't have plans for Christmas Eve, nor Christmas.

And he really didn't want to be alone during what should be a joyous time. He stood at the back door, looking at all the snow, the path he'd tromped through it to get to the farm, thinking, *Then do something about it.*

He wanted to call Amanda, as she'd mentioned several traditions at Whiskey Mountain Lodge. He'd love to have a private dinner with just her.

Or he could organize an event for anyone with nowhere else to go right here at his house. He could bake ham and make potatoes, and order rolls and pies.

Yes, that was what he'd do, and he reached for his phone to call the pastor so the word could be spread.

CHAPTER 21

"I do *not* want to be set up again," Amanda said, loading her breakfast dishes into the dishwasher.

"Fine," Graham said. "You're still coming to the tree lighting, though, right?"

"Of course," she said. "I've attended alone before, believe it or not."

"Mom, I think you should call Finn."

Amanda straightened, her thoughts already tangled. "I can't do that."

"Why not?" Graham asked. "He was down here yesterday, you know. He looked miserable, and I heard him talking to Laney about the saddles. He said he probably won't need any more for a while."

"Why is that significant?" she asked. She knew Finn bought saddles from Laney, but she wasn't entirely sure why.

"He said he's selling a lot of his horses. Not getting new ones. No horses. No saddles."

Amanda moved over to the door, trying to riddle out what it all meant. "I miss him," she whispered.

"I know you do, Mom," Graham said, and she suddenly remembered she was on the phone with him. "Why don't you just tell me what happened?"

"I don't know what happened."

"You won't tell Beau either, and it's obvious to everyone you're in love with him."

Amanda shook her head. "He doesn't live here," she said. "And I can't give up the house." There, she'd said it. "He wanted me to move to Dog Valley with him, and I... can't."

Graham sighed into the phone. "Mom, I'm sorry, but that's just ridiculous."

"What?" she asked, her pulse skipping.

"You don't need to sell your house." Graham started laughing, but Amanda couldn't figure out what was so funny. "So keep the house, Mom. I don't see why you can't have the house *and* Finn."

She opened her mouth to say something, but nothing came to her mind. Eventually, she said, "And what? The house sits empty?"

"No," Graham said slowly. "I know someone who could use it while you're away. Fill it with family and have celebrations there. Just the kind you want, like the one you had at Thanksgiving."

"Graham," she said, a sigh following. "I know you

bought the lodge...I mean, I know you didn't buy the lodge to take those times from me."

"I really didn't, Mother," he said. "I didn't even know that's what had happened. I'm sorry." It wasn't the first time he'd apologized since Thanksgiving, and Amanda hated that she'd caused him turmoil.

She lifted her head. "Who needs the house?"

"Eli," he said. "He wants to come home."

Her eyebrows went up. "He does? Why hasn't he said anything?"

"Oh, he's still making up his mind. But the resort bores him, and Meg wants to be closer to family." Graham chuckled, but Amanda's hopes soared.

"I want the house to stay in the family," she said.

"Give it to Eli, then," Graham said. "Or Andrew. Heaven knows he and Becca are going to have the most children."

"You think so?"

"Mom, the rest of us are done."

"What?" She spun from the winter landscape beyond the window. "You are?"

"Laney says she's too old to have more babies, and her last pregnancy was very difficult. We have Bailey and Ronnie. That's who we're getting."

"Beau?"

"Lily's older than Laney, Mom."

"And Meg can't have kids." Amanda nodded, unsure of how she hadn't thought about this before. "They could adopt more children."

LIZ ISAACSON

"I think they will," Graham said. "But it's Andrew who'll give you all the grandbabies. And they live in that tiny house in town. Give your place to him. Or have him buy it. You know we're all billionaires, right?"

Amanda smiled, but he was right. She didn't need to sell her house. She just wanted to keep it. Wanted to be able to feel the love she'd felt there so often.

"And Mom? Call Finn. Call him and invite him to the tree lighting and Christmas celebrations at the lodge." Something crashed on his end, and he said, "I have to go. Love you, Mom."

The line went dead, and Amanda let her hand fall to her side. *Call Finn.*

She had no idea how to do that. Would he even answer?

She busied her hands with wiping down an already clean countertop, her mind spinning, spinning, and spinning around Finn.

Before she knew it, she was behind the wheel of her SUV, pointing it toward Dog Valley. Her fingers gripped the wheel too tightly as she drove, and she had no idea what to say to Finn once she arrived.

But she knew the way, and she pulled into his driveway to see a thin trail of smoke coming from the chimney. So he was home, or he had been.

"Not going to see him sitting out here," she muttered to herself, but she couldn't seem to get out of the vehicle.

She had no words to say to him, and she couldn't

196

imagine he would welcome her here. After all, hadn't she turned Jason away in a situation similar to this one?

Before she could get out or back away from the house, his truck pulled in beside her. As if in slow motion, she turned to look at him, and their eyes met across the space and through the windows separating them.

All she could do was look at him, and then she jumped out of her SUV and started around the front of his truck, winter's cold bite not nearly as savage as she remembered it being.

"Finn," she said as he got out of the truck. "I'm so sorry, Finn." She didn't have anything for him. She should've brought cookies or soup or something.

All she had was herself, and she was suddenly not good enough.

"What are you doing here?" he asked as if she hadn't spoken. He moved to the back of the truck and let the tailgate down so his dogs could get out. They jumped down, except for the black Lab, and Finn helped Licorice to the ground.

"What happened to him?" she asked, noticing the wrapped paw and the way the dog limped.

"He got stuck in a fence," Finn said, barely looking at her again. He started for the house and opened the door for the canines, who ran inside. He turned back, but Amanda had paused at the bottom of the steps, so unsure.

"Do you want to come in?" he asked.

She reached for the railing and used it to pull herself

up. "Yes." She stepped past him, and he entered last, closing the door behind them.

"You're not dating anyone new, are you?" she asked, his home as warm and welcoming as she remembered it.

He gave a scoff and a mirthless laugh. "I think that's a question for you, Amanda." He moved past her, once again barely looking at her. She detected only coldness from him, but she reminded herself that he'd invited her in. He hadn't demanded she leave, the way she had when Jason had come back, begging for a second chance.

Her mind seized on those words. "I want a second chance," she said. "Finn." She followed him into the kitchen, where he stood at the back door, letting the dogs outside again.

"Finn," she said again, almost desperate for him to understand. She'd had plenty of time to find the right words to say to him, and yet they still weren't there.

"I want you more than the house," she blurted. "Will you please look at me?"

He turned from the door as it drifted closed, his bright, ocean-colored eyes sparking.

She swallowed. "I love you. And I love my house. And I want both things. I don't need to sell my house. One of my sons is going to live in it. I want to be here, at the farm with you." Amanda took a step forward and paused. "Graham seems to think you won't have horses soon."

"I've sold almost all of them," Finn confirmed, straightening his cowboy hat. "Truth is, Amanda, I didn't want the farm if you weren't going to come to it. So I've been making plans to return to Kentucky."

She blinked, sure she'd heard him wrong. "Kentucky? You said you'd never go back."

"Yeah, well, that was before."

"Before what?"

"Before I couldn't stand to be in the same state as you."

Tears filled her eyes, and she shook her head. "I'm so sorry. Finn, I really am." She crossed the room to him and cradled his face in both of her hands. "Please forgive me. I'm sorry."

Finn searched her face, so much stubbornness in his. "I don't want to go back to Kentucky," he whispered.

"Then don't," she said just as quietly.

"Was it really just the house?" he asked. "Because it seemed to me that you were clinging to a little more than that."

"I think I was," she said, grateful he brought his arms around her. She felt safe in the circle of his arms. Loved. "But I'm learning how to let go. I just need a strong cowboy to catch me." She tried a smile, rejoicing when Finn returned it.

"You don't like the farm," he said next.

"I like it fine," she said. "Because you like it."

"We can go to your church."

"It's a long drive every Sunday."

"It's not that bad," he said. "I've been doing it, and honestly, it's not that bad."

"Will you come to the lodge for Christmas?" she asked.

"I thought you'd never ask," he said, swiping his cowboy hat off his head and leaning down to kiss her.

Pure happiness flowed through Amanda, and she tried to pour everything she felt into this kiss with Finn. "I really am sorry," she said. "I just...I don't know. I think in the back of my mind, I never thought I'd find someone else to love. And then I did, and I didn't know what to do with that."

"Mm." Finn held onto her and swayed. "I want you to come to Kentucky with me," he said. "I'm going on the twenty-seventh. My sister and her husband will be there. My mom and dad."

Surprise flowed through her. "Really?"

"I didn't want to spend the holidays alone," he said. "I was organizing a meal here, but I'll call the pastor and cancel it."

"You don't have to do that," she said.

"I really want to be at the lodge with your family." He touched his lips to her jaw. "Okay?"

She held onto his shoulders and allowed the sweet feelings of love and peace move through her. "Okay. And yes, I'd love to go to Kentucky to meet your family."

"Perfect," he said before kissing her again.

CHAPTER 22

F inn pulled up to Amanda's house to pick her up for the tree lighting ceremony taking place up at Whiskey Mountain Lodge. He was early, but that didn't stop him from going up the steps and knocking on the front door. They'd agreed to have a small gift exchange at her place, and Finn's nerves fired at sixty miles per hour while he waited on the porch.

"Hey," she said, opening the door. They'd been back together for a couple of weeks, and he'd spent a lot of time here with her, talking. Apparently, her third son was returning to Coral Canyon and would be living in her home.

If he'd have known she just wanted to keep the house, he'd have bought it from her. It seemed so simple now, and yet he'd thought there had been more at play. He'd asked her a few times, and she'd insisted she didn't have any other qualms about being with him.

He hoped she'd been telling the truth, because he had a diamond in his pocket and didn't want to be down on one knee when another issue came to his attention.

Maybe you should wait to ask her, he thought as he stepped inside. Amanda closed the door behind him, linked her arm through his, and said, "Are you ready for the craziness at the lodge?"

"You know me," he said. "I love craziness."

She laughed, the sound like music to his ears. "Okay, so I got you something, and I hope you like it." She moved over to the Christmas tree they'd decorated together. He'd pulled it out of her garage for her, and he'd replaced the burnt-out bulbs, stood on the ladder to get the top right, and enjoyed spending the afternoon with her, making new memories in this house.

Of course, he wanted her in his house too, and she'd brought her stocking to his place, as she'd wanted to spend Christmas Eve with him there.

She bent to pick up a big box. "Did you want to go first?" she asked.

"No." Finn shook his head, wishing he had a back-up plan. Another gift. But he didn't.

"Did you bring something?" She looked at him, concern running through her eyes. "I thought we were exchanging gifts."

"I have something," he said, crossing over to her. "It's just not as big as yours."

She smiled and handed him the package. "Don't be

impressed. Do you know how hard it is to buy something for someone who has everything?"

"Yeah, I have no idea what that's like," he said dryly. He sat down on the couch, thinking this package sure was big for how little it weighed. She joined him on the couch, and Finn took a moment to look at her.

"I sure do love you," he said, his heartbeat already starting to hammer. He hoped he'd be able to give her the reaction she wanted when he opened this present.

Amanda kissed him, grounding him in his decision to propose to her that evening. He kissed her back, stealing some of her strength, before focusing on the present. "Okay, let's see what we've got."

He ripped off the brightly colored paper and found a box for a slow cooker beneath it. "I know that's not it," he said, chuckling. He peeled off the tape on the top flaps and looked inside. A single piece of paper sat at the bottom, and he glanced at her and then reached for it.

"What's this?" His fingers touched more than one paper, and he scrabbled around to pick them all up.

"Okay, so it's a bacon-of-the-month club," she started.

"I haven't even looked at them yet," he said.

"Sorry." She grinned at him, and Finn smiled back at her.

"Bacon-of-the-month club," he said, reading the top one. "Sounds delicious." He flipped to the next one. "Harvest Bounty, a cooking box delivered weekly."

"I'm going to come make you dinner every week with

that one. They send out seasonal vegetables and all kinds of proteins. It looked really good."

Warmth spread through Finn. "You're going to come cook for me?"

"Yes."

He cradled her face and kissed her again. "Thank you."

"You didn't even look at all of them."

"Right." He moved Harvest Bounty to the back. "Jerky-of-the-month."

"I know you love that stuff, and you can take it with you out on the farm."

"Both true." Another flip. "Chocolate-of-the-month. A dessert package filled with delicious sweets."

"That's another cooking box," she said. "But with desserts. I'm going to come make those too."

He made it back to the bacon certificate, his heart full. "It's a long drive to make brownies," he said.

"I know," she said. "But I'm going to be doing it anyway."

"I can come to you," he said, ducking his head. If he got his way with the diamond, though, they'd be married before next Christmas. In fact, he couldn't imagine *not* being married before next Christmas.

"Finn, it won't be a long drive for very long. Eli and Meg are moving into the house at the end of January."

His heart leapt. "Maybe you can move to Dog Valley then."

"That's what I was thinking. Surely there are places to rent there."

"Actually," he said, pulling his Christmas gift for her from his pocket. "Maybe you won't need to rent." He revealed the silver-wrapped box, the navy blue bow a little crushed, and handed it to her.

"Finn Barber," she said, her voice mostly air.

"Open it." He needed a few seconds to gather his thoughts anyway.

She delicately pulled on the bow, releasing it. The lid came off easily then, and she cracked open the black velvet box where the diamond lay next. She stared at the ring, her chin wobbling the slightest bit.

When she lifted her eyes to his, they were filled with tears.

"Don't cry, beautiful," he said. "I'm in love with you, and I figured we're both getting older and there's no need to wait to get married. I mean, I *will* wait if that's what you want, but I want you beside me, in *our* house, in Dog Valley, as soon as possible."

He gently pushed her hair off her face and kissed her carefully. "What do you think? Will you marry me?"

She nodded, her forehead bumping his. "Yes, Finn. I'll marry you."

He kissed her again, this time with more passion and abandon. "Merry Christmas, Amanda."

"Merry Christmas, Finn."

AN HOUR LATER, she led him into the lodge, a wall of

noise hitting him squarely in the chest. He'd been there before, of course, but now the living room boasted a gigantic tree that stretched all the way toward the vaulted, two-story ceiling.

Someone had done a masterful job decorating it, and he could only gaze at the tree in wonder. Though it wasn't lit yet, it was still majestic and beautiful.

Laughter rang out from the kitchen, and Amanda went that way. Finn stuck close to her, wondering if she'd make a big announcement for their engagement or not. They hadn't talked about it, instead taking the time to choose a date.

February twentieth. Only two months from now. She said she could live here at the lodge or stay in her house even after Eli and Meg moved in until then. Finn hadn't argued with her. He just wanted her with him on the farm.

"Hey, Mom," Graham said, and Finn let go of Amanda's hand so she could embrace her son. She went around and said hello to everyone, and Finn followed her lead once again. Shaking hands and smiling, he truly felt welcome and loved in this lodge.

"What in the world is this?" Laney asked, her voice much too loud. "Amanda."

Finn turned to find Laney had gripped Amanda's left hand. With wide eyes, she kept looking back and forth from her hand to her face. "Graham, look at what your mother is wearing." She lifted Amanda's arm as if Graham couldn't see the diamond from where he stood a few feet away.

It wasn't that small. In fact, in Finn's opinion, the diamond was huge.

Graham turned to Finn, who could only smile at his fiancée.

"Finn and I are engaged," Amanda said, her whole face lighting up.

A beat of silence followed, only to be drowned out by a roar of laughter and congratulations after that.

Finn hugged anyone who came near, and he accepted the cup of coffee Celia passed to him.

"All right, all right," Amanda finally said, holding up her hands. "Let's go light this tree so we can eat." She stepped into Finn's side, and he curled his arm around her waist and pressed his lips to her temple.

They followed the others into the living room, where Graham had saved them a couple of seats on the couch as Beau stood near the fireplace. "Welcome to the lodge, everyone." He smiled around at everyone. "We're glad to be expanding our ranks again this year. Welcome to the family officially, Finn."

"Thank you," he said, his heart expanding a few sizes.

Beau looked around the room. "Any other announcements? We know Andrew and Becca have a new baby coming. Fran and Jack are going to Egypt in March."

"Eli and Meg are moving into my house at the end of January," Amanda said.

Beau nodded and said, "That's right."

"We have news," Vi Christopherson said, looking at her husband. "And so does Rose."

Finn had heard all the stories of how the two Everett sisters were married on the same day, and how even though they weren't Amanda's blood daughters-in-law, she loved them like they were.

"I'm having two girls," Vi said.

Lily gasped, her eyes round. "You found out? You said nothing."

"Mom knew."

"Mom?" Lily asked.

Fran Everett nodded and wiped her tears. "And Rose—"

"Mom," Rose practically yelled, looking at her and then her husband, Liam. "Do you want to tell them?"

Liam looked supremely uncomfortable, but he cleared his throat. "Rose is having triplets."

"Triplets, oh my goodness," Amanda said, getting up and going over to Rose to give her a hug.

Finn just basked in the family atmosphere in the lodge. He'd never felt anything like it, and he suddenly understood what Amanda had meant about the magic here.

"Okay," Beau said several minutes later. "I think it's time to light the tree." He looked at Lily, who couldn't seem to stop crying. "And I think we'll change up who we were going to ask. Lily?"

She stood, her baby perched on her hip. "Rose, you win the day. Triplets." She shook her head. "Get yourself up here and flip this switch."

The blonde woman laughed as she moved to the front

of the room. She positioned her hand on the switch and said, "Ready?"

"Ready," everyone chorused back—everyone except Finn, but he'd be ready next year.

She flipped the switch, and the Christmas tree burst into white light. The sight of it took his breath away, and Finn could only sit and experience the happiness and joy Amanda's family had brought into his life.

She leaned into his side, and he kneaded her closer. "Best tradition ever," she sighed, and Finn couldn't agree more.

CHAPTER 23

F inn's nervous energy infiltrated Amanda's senses, and she wanted to reassure him that he'd be fine. But she wasn't the one who'd left home and never returned. She'd taken the boys and Ron back to Dallas every year for a long time. Now, only her father was still alive, and he lived with her younger sister.

She'd called and invited them all to the wedding in February, but the weather wouldn't be great then. Wendy had said she'd bring their dad though, and Amanda had made arrangements for them to stay at the lodge.

In fact, she was getting married at the lodge. She and Ron had been married in the church where she'd gone forever, and she wanted something different for her and Finn. Pastor Franklin would still come do the ceremony, and she'd have a small, family-only dinner at her favorite restaurant in town, Scratched.

She reached for Finn's hand as they walked through

the airport. He squeezed her fingers, and his tension lessened. They got their bags and went through the line to rent the car. He drove, the action as easy here as it was in Dog Valley where he'd lived for so long.

"Is this place familiar?" she asked, noting all the farms, the barns and horses everywhere.

"Yes," he said.

"Good or bad?"

"It just is," he said. "This place hasn't grown much. It'll be nice to see my sister."

"I'm excited to meet them all," she said as he turned onto a lane bordered with white fences.

"Won't be long now," he said, nodding. "Those are our fences. My dad's fences."

"They have B's on them," she said.

"Yep." Finn didn't say anything else, and she wasn't sure if the monogrammed fences bothered him or not. He'd always followed her lead with her family, and she was determined to do the same for him.

"She's going to try to feed us all the time," Finn said. "That's how my mother shows she cares. Food."

"Well, I *am* hungry," Amanda said.

"Good," he said. "She'll probably have a seven-course meal ready. Well, not her. But the chef. She has a chef."

"Graham pays Celia to cook for our family." To Amanda, that wasn't that big of a deal.

Finn just nodded, his eyes trained out the windshield. Several minutes later, he pulled up to a sprawling house that made hers look like a child's dollhouse. "Holy cow, Finn." She gazed at it, sure she'd be getting lost there.

"I told you," he said. "You were supposed to Google it."

"I wanted to be surprised." And she was. A woman came out of the front doors, gliding between the pillars, wearing a beautiful red dress.

"My mother," he said. "She likes to dress up. I don't think I mentioned that."

"It looks like she's ready to welcome a king," Amanda said, drawing in a sharp breath. "You also didn't tell me to dress up."

"That's because you don't need to." He indicated his own clothes. "I'm wearing jeans, Amanda. You're fine. More than fine."

She didn't feel fine. She felt very out of place, and she wondered if Finn felt like this with her sons and grandchildren. She was definitely going to ask him the first chance she got.

"Stay here," he said. "At least let me show my mother I have some Southern manners left, okay?" He grinned at her and got out of the car, circling around the front to open her door for her.

Amanda took his hand to get out and then she hooked her arm through his. "I'm going to fall down."

"It's a flat surface," he said. "Look who's nervous now."

"I'm sorry," she said. "I just wasn't expecting the dress."

"Hey, Mom," he said as they climbed the steps. He let go of Amanda to hug his mother, who cried right there on his shoulder.

"Come on now," she heard him say, but his voice sounded a bit choked too.

"You came home," she finally said as she stepped back. "I just can't believe it." She took her son's face in her hands and smiled through her tears.

When she turned her attention to Amanda, it was with the brightest smile on the planet. "Mom," Finn said. "This is my fiancée, Amanda Whittaker."

"Amanda Whittaker," his mother said as if she really were the Queen of England. "How very nice to meet you."

"You too," she said, moving effortlessly into the hug.

"Okay, Mom," Finn said, chuckling, but she didn't release Amanda. "Amanda, this is my mom, Trudy."

She stepped back then, and Amanda kept her smile in place. "Welcome to our home," she said. "Rhonda's in the kitchen, Finny. Let's go say hello."

"Where's Dad?" Finn asked, taking Amanda's hand again as another man came outside.

"Jasper will get the bags," Trudy said, and Amanda watched the well-dressed man head toward the car.

"You never said where Dad was," Finn said as they went inside. Amanda couldn't take in all the grandeur at once, but Finn didn't even look at it. She didn't understand how someone as...simple and unpretentious as him had come from all of this.

"He's in Nashville," Trudy said. "Won't be back until tomorrow night."

"Mom," Finn said with warning in his voice. "Why's he in Nashville? I wanted to talk to him. Have him meet Amanda."

"And you will," Trudy said airily. "You're not leaving until the day after that."

Finn exchanged a glance with Amanda, and she tore her eyes from the artwork to give him the best smile she had.

"Finny!" A woman launched herself out of the kitchen. Finn laughed with his full voice as he hugged his sister. "And oh, my goodness. Finn has a new woman." Rhonda latched onto Amanda's hand, and she once again wondered what cloth Finn had been cut from. He didn't seem to belong to his family at all.

"Amanda, my older sister Rhonda. Her husband, Jones."

"Nice to meet you both," Amanda said, accepting hugs and cheek kisses from everyone.

"Who's hungry?" Trudy asked, and Finn just looked at Amanda again.

She couldn't help laughing at the same time she said, "I am, Mrs. Barber."

"Oh, please," Trudy said. "I am not Mrs. Barber. Trudy is fine." She took the lid off a pot and added, "I think this is the soup."

"Mom," Rhonda said. "Let's go into the dining room."

She steered her mother through a double set of doors, and Amanda linked her arm through Finn's again.

"Yes, let's eat," he said, causing Amanda to laugh again.

⚜

THE FOLLOWING EVENING, Finn invited Amanda out to the stables. She went, because she'd spent the last day and a half hearing about them. Seeing them was radically different than the images she had in her mind.

"These horses live better than I do," she said, and Finn nodded.

"That they do."

"Do your horses live like this in Dog Valley?"

"Yes, ma'am," he said, stopping outside a closed stall. This one had doors that went all the way to the ceiling, as if someone might turn to stone if they caught a glimpse of the horse within. A chalkboard hanging on the door had a star on it.

"What does that mean?" she asked.

"This is Dad's star horse this year," he said. "He'll fetch the highest price. See the date there?" He indicated some tiny numbers Amanda hadn't noticed. "That's the auction date. This is Stars For Eyes, who Rhonda was talking about last night."

"Oh, the one who came from the other winners."

"That's right. Running is in the genes," he said. "It's

why we pay so much for stud fees." He flashed her a smile that she could tell pinched along the edges.

"What are you going to say to him?" she asked. They'd talked a little bit about his father, but Finn usually only said two or three sentences before the conversation topic wearied him. She knew Finn had left for college, promising to come back—and he had. But only for six months, and then he'd stormed out of Kentucky and hadn't been back in a very, very long time.

"I'm going to apologize," Finn said. "And hope he forgives me."

Amanda's heart expanded for the goodness of this man. "I'm sure he will."

"My dad isn't a very tolerant man," he said. "And his old age has only made him more stubborn." He wandered down the aisle to a horse who poked his head over the half-closed door. Even Amanda found comfort in the horses now, and she ran her fingers down the side of this one's face.

He easily stood a couple of feet taller than her, and she could see him flying around the racetrack. "If there's one thing I know about getting older," she said. "It's that I might be set in my ways, but I'm more open to love too."

She gave him a smile, and Finn put his arm around her and leaned his face against her shoulder. "Thank you for coming here with me."

"Of course."

"It was not easy for me to come."

"But you did."

"Yeah," he said. "I guess even old dogs can learn new tricks."

Amanda kissed him, hoping he'd take some of her calmness for his own. "He should be here by now, shouldn't he?"

"Yes," Finn said. "Let's go see if he's arrived." He'd taken three steps toward the door, just securing her hand in his, when he froze. "Dad."

A big bear of a man stood in the doorway, a cowboy hat obscuring most of his face. Amanda couldn't tell if he was smiling or frowning, and all the oxygen felt like it had been removed from the air.

Finn strode toward his father, the speed of his steps increasing the closer he got. He threw his arms around him and said, "I'm sorry, Dad. I'm so sorry."

Amanda pressed one palm over her heart as it beat wildly beneath her breastbone. She knew exactly what that apology felt like as it came out of her mouth, knew the desperation behind every word, every letter.

And the best part was that Finn's father put his arms around his son and embraced him. "It's okay, son," he said. "It's okay."

FEBRUARY 20

Finn stamped the snow from his boots as he reached the deck. The cold felt brutal against his tongue, the back of his throat, and all the way down into his lungs.

Didn't matter.

He was getting married today.

Inside the back door, he waited for his three Labs to enter, and then he pressed the door closed and locked it. "Zach's going to be by later," he told them. "So everyone just take a nap this morning, okay?"

None of the dogs answered him, of course, and Finn couldn't nap. He did have time for a cup of coffee and to get in the shower. As he poured a cup of coffee, his dad came down the hall from the guest room.

"Morning, Dad," he said. "Coffee?"

"Yes."

Finn slid his mug to his dad, who started spooning sugar into the brew. "Is Mom up?"

"Yep."

Finn poured another cup of coffee and added sugar and cream to his. "You guys can get to the lodge okay? I need to be there a little bit early."

"Your mom wants to come with you," he said. "She doesn't think we need to leave your truck there. We'll drive it back here."

"That's fine," he said. They'd talked through a couple of different scenarios, one being him leaving his truck at the lodge and one being his parents driving it back to Dog Valley for their last night in town. "Zach's on chores tonight, but you're more than welcome to go out with him."

His parents had been at his farm for a week now, and his dad had actually praised him for how he had things running here. Finn had never been prouder than when his dad complimented his henhouse and examined the horse Finn had chosen as his star for the year.

"All right," his dad said, and Finn excused himself to shower. With his coffee gone and everything washed, he threw his suitcase onto the seat beside him and laid his tuxedo over that.

"Mom," he said as he went back into the house. She poked her head around the corner, using both hands to put her earrings in. "We need to go."

"Five minutes," she said. "Daddy's just getting

dressed." She finished with her earring and beamed at Finn as she approached him. "You look so handsome."

"I've been married before, Mom. Don't make this into a big deal."

"It is a big deal," she said. "You've been alone for so long, and now you don't have to be. I won't be nearly as worried knowing Amanda is here with you." She grinned at him and straightened his collar, though he'd be changing once he got to the lodge.

"I'm glad you and Dad could come." His sister was staying at a hotel in Coral Canyon, and she had to rush out after the wedding as her son's wife was about to give birth to her second grandchild.

Finn was about to get six grandchildren the moment he said, "I do." And he couldn't wait.

His father finally came around the corner, tugging on his shirtsleeves. "They're too short," he grumbled.

"That's what you get when you won't go to the tailor," his mother said, her nose practically ten stories up. Finn ducked his head and said nothing, remembering his dress hat at the very last moment, and only because it sat on the back of the couch—right where Amanda had put it.

"Let me move my stuff to the back," he said. "I forgot you were riding with me." Nerves dodged through him as he threw his suitcase and tuxedo in the back seat. "Okay, get in."

The drive to Whiskey Mountain Lodge took a few extra minutes, simply because Mother Nature had decided yesterday would be a great day to drop thirteen inches of snow on the state of Wyoming.

Flights had been delayed, but everyone Amanda wanted at the wedding had made it to town. Now Finn just needed to get there.

The parking lot seemed abnormally full when he arrived, and he pulled under the overhang in the circle drive. If he thought he'd seen chaos at the lodge before—and he had—it was nothing like today.

"Ma!" Beau yelled. "Your groom is here." He took the garment bag from Finn and added in a much quieter voice. "Hullo, Finn. Good to see you." He glanced at Finn's parents. "Welcome to Whiskey Mountain Lodge, Barbers. I'm Beau." He grinned and took their coats. "They might be able to put you to work in the kitchen."

His mother led his father in that direction, but Finn stayed by the front door as Amanda came around the corner. She hugged his mom and tipped up on her toes to give his father a kiss on the cheek, and then she beelined for him.

"What's wrong?" he asked, noting the anxious look on her face.

"I didn't want to say anything," she said. "But I feel so stupid."

"What?" Finn received her into his arms, not really worried about what the problem was. She was here. He was here. No matter what it was, they could still get married.

"I ordered your ring from the jeweler, and he

promised me it would be here on time. But the storm kept it from getting delivered." She pulled back and looked into his face, pure concern in her pretty eyes. "I'm so sorry."

Finn smiled at her and bent down to kiss her. "I don't care about a ring," he said, brushing his lips against hers. "You're here, right?" He kissed her again, holding on longer this time. "Still going to say yes?"

She smiled. "Yes."

"The ring is trivial," he said.

"Mom," Graham said, drawing her attention. "You can use this." He hurried across the room and held something out to his mother.

She took it, examining it for a moment. "Graham, this is made out of twist ties."

"I know," he said, grinning. "Bailey and Stockton made it."

Finn caught the two grandchildren huddled near the doorway, and he nudged Amanda so she'd see them too. She glanced in that direction and gestured for them to come closer.

The two kids ran over, and she bent down to give them simultaneous hugs. "It's a ring, Grandma," Stockton said. "It works, right?"

"Of course it does," Amanda said, and Finn's heart filled with love.

He crouched down too, though the action hurt his knees. "Thanks, you guys."

The two kids hugged him too, and he closed his eyes in

LIZ ISAACSON

a moment of pure joy. Stockton pulled back. "Can I call you Grandpa now?"

"No," Amanda said, swatting at him. "Not until after the wedding." She laughed, and nudged Stockton and Bailey away from Finn. "Now go find your mothers. You're not even ready for the wedding yet."

"You're not wearing your dress yet, either, Grandma," Bailey said, her eyes round and thoughtful.

"That's because I don't want Finn to see me in it," she said, straightening.

Finn accepted Graham's strong hand to help him up, and he watched the kids skip away. "I guess we better go get ready," Finn said.

"Yeah," Graham said. "I have you upstairs, Finn. Follow me." He moved around the bannister and started upstairs. Finn collected his garment bag and kissed Amanda on the cheek. "See you soon."

Graham led him to the first room on the right and held open the door. "Here you go."

"Thanks, Graham." Finn paused and looked at the other man. "For everything."

"Who knew a blind date would lead to this?" Graham grinned at him. "I'm so happy for you two. You deserve the world." He shook Finn's hand, quickly pulling him into a hug.

"Welcome to the family, Finn." Graham left, and Finn took a moment to just appreciate the moment.

"Thank you," he whispered to the Lord. He dressed

224

quickly and stayed in the room until Graham returned for him.

The living room had been transformed, and he stood next to the pastor on the step right beside the front door. He'd barely taken his position when Amanda appeared, her dress simple and beautiful, a bunch of pink and yellow roses in her hand.

Everything fell away after that. The fussy babies. The oohs and ahhs. The tears and sniffling. All he could see and hear was Amanda. And when she slid that ring made of twist ties on his finger, gratitude and love exploded through him.

"I love you," she whispered.

Emotion choked in Finn's throat, but he managed to say, "And I love you," before the pastor pronounced them married, and he was able to kiss her for the first time as his wife.

The End

SNEAK PEEK! HER COWBOY BILLIONAIRE BEST MAN CHAPTER ONE

Celia Armstrong ducked out of the kitchen at Whiskey Mountain Lodge, glad this wedding had been scheduled in the winter. Because, wow. This kitchen radiated with heat from all the cooking she'd been doing.

Her hair felt flat and lifeless, and she moved down the hall toward the guest bathroom in Beau and Lily's suite. The lodge seemed stuffed with noise, and it actually warmed Celia's heart. Her house was entirely too quiet these days, and she loved coming up to Whiskey Mountain Lodge and spending time with the Whittakers.

In the bathroom, she spruced up her hair and pulled a tube of lip gloss out of her purse. With perfectly pink and shiny lips, she finally felt ready to attend a wedding. And not just any wedding. Her best friend's wedding.

Amanda Whittaker had been dating for several years, and she'd finally found the perfect cowboy for her. Of course, she'd never really been looking for a cowboy, and Celia hadn't been looking at all.

"You should be," she murmured to her reflection, wondering when her hair had gotten quite so gray. She was fifty-five now, and Brandon had died twenty years ago. Celia had been right in the thick of raising her two daughters, and she hadn't needed anything or anyone else.

There hadn't been *time* for anything or anyone else. With a five-year-old and a one-year-old, Celia had often felt like she was drowning.

But her daughters were both grown now, both in college, and both living somewhere else.

Maybe it's time, she thought, her eyes pressing closed in a long blink. A sense of peace came over her, and she tipped her chin toward the ceiling, imagining her thoughts could get all the way to heaven.

"Dear Lord," she began, the way she had for many years when she had no idea what to do. How to get Reagan's fever down. How to get Ruth to eat something more than chicken nuggets.

"Could I find another husband?" she asked, hoping the Lord would send a direct sign to her eyes and ears.

Of course, He didn't. She'd learned over the years that His plans for her were much more subtle. Sometimes she wondered if He was even there, and then He would remind her in powerful ways that He was.

Someone knocked on the door. "Hey, Celia," Beau said, his voice light and carefree. "Um, there's a problem in the kitchen...."

"What did you boys touch?" she asked, giving him a smile as she stepped past him into the hall.

"Nothing, I swear," he said. "Someone asked for coffee, and I've seen Graham pour coffee before. But the mug cracked, and now there's some sort of problem."

Celia heard the commotion coming from the kitchen, and she wondered what had possessed Amanda to choose the lodge to get married. It was a huge building, sure. Many bedrooms upstairs, a few downstairs, and a theater room. The kitchen and dining room took up a third of the main level, and the master suite took up another third, leaving only a third for a living room where the ceremony would take place in half an hour.

Who needed coffee thirty minutes before a wedding?

She rounded the corner into the kitchen to find Graham and Laney there, each holding a towel. "It's fine," Graham said when he saw her. "We didn't touch the food, and nothing got damaged."

Celia's eyes still swept the trays and trays of appetizers she'd spent many hours prepping. Nothing seemed out of the ordinary, and she finally looked back at Graham.

"Why'd you go get her?" Graham asked Beau, taking off his hat and running his hands through his hair. He wore a tuxedo, and he didn't seem super happy about it. But he'd do anything for his mother, Celia knew that. He threw the coffee-stained towel in the kitchen sink, and Celia moved to get it.

She took the one from Laney too and said, "It's fine, Graham. Is everything ready for the wedding?"

"It better be," Laney said with a grateful smile. "Everything looks great, Celia."

"Thanks. I'm just going to put these in the washing machine." Celia slipped out of the kitchen again, unsure as to why all these people here were causing so much anxiety to trip through her.

She loved having a houseful of people, and she'd thrived on the Christmas Eve meals here for the past eight years. Why she felt so lonely today, she wasn't sure. A sigh leaked from her mouth as she tossed the towels in the washing machine and stayed in the quiet laundry room.

The sound of the back door opening, and a couple of male voices, indicated two men had just come in from outside. One man chuckled. Celia turned and caught a glimpse of him as he moved past the entrance to the laundry room, but he also wore a black jacket across those broad shoulders, black slacks, as well as a charcoal-colored cowboy hat.

Celia had grown up in Wyoming and spent her whole life in the presence of cowboys. They were her kryptonite, and she wondered if the man walking with Finn was single. He'd brought a friend to the wedding, as well as his daughters and their boyfriends.

So maybe....

The man paused in the doorway and turned toward Finn, providing Celia with a nice profile, what with that strong jaw and full lips.

He looked a little bit familiar to her. How that was

possible, she didn't know. She'd lived in Coral Canyon so long, she knew everyone. Of course, so had Amanda, and she'd found a new husband in Dog Valley.

And this guy was talking to Finn. Perhaps he lived in the small town thirty minutes north of Coral Canyon too.

He glanced back the way he'd come, and Celia's heart started bouncing around inside her chest. He was extremely handsome, and a smile touched his mouth as he followed Finn and left Celia's eyesight.

Alone, she pressed one palm to her pulse, almost willing it to calm down.

She was definitely ready to start dating again, and she thought, *Thank You, Lord,* before heading down the hall after that handsome cowboy toward the living room. After all, her best friend was about to get married.

Before she could take too many steps, really get a good look at that cowboy who'd accelerated her pulse with a chuckle and a smile, someone called her name. A fair bit of panic rode in the two syllables, and she hurried back into the kitchen to find Stockton standing in the middle of a couple dozen tarts.

Eli's face looked like he'd been stung by an army of red ants. His face shone with anger, the bright red so not like him. "Stockton," he barked. "I told you not to come in here."

"It's fine," Celia said, though she had no time to make more tarts. It was fine. They could make everything work with less.

"I'll pick them up," Stockton said, his voice high-pitched and tinny. The boy had just turned eleven, and he and his parents and sister had just moved back to Coral Canyon three weeks ago. He stooped, his perfectly polished shoe squishing a cherry tart.

"Stockton." Eli sounded one breath away from losing it completely.

Celia looked at him and stepped between him and the child and said, "Eli, it was an accident. I'll take him to clean up. Could you get these in the trashcan, please?"

His face crumbled. "Celia—"

"It's fine." She glanced over as Beau appeared in the doorway. "Beau will help you." She pointed to the floor. "Clean this up. Your mother doesn't need to know."

Beau's jaw clenched, and he nodded. Celia turned, put her arm around Stockton, and said, "Take off your shoe, Stocky."

He did, and Celia took it. "This will clean up easily." She wished all the windows were open, as she felt so dang hot. "Come on, baby," she said, and Stockton swiped at his face as he spun and marched out of the kitchen, his gait uneven with only one polished, black shoe on his feet.

She followed him back to the bathroom where she'd freshened up. She felt like no amount of lip gloss could conceal how harried and stressed she was.

"I'm sorry, Celia," Stockton said, his tears still brimming in those innocent eyes.

"It's fine," she said. "They're tarts. No big deal." She glanced at him as she bent to get a washcloth out of the vanity. "Did your dad tell you to stay out of the kitchen?"

"Yeah." Stockton looked miserable. "But me and Bailey just wanted to run down to the barn real quick."

"Your grandmother is getting married in ten minutes. You thought you had time to get down to the barn real quick?" She turned on the water and smiled at the boy. "I miss you, bud." She gathered him into a hug, suddenly anxious for her own grandchildren. "I'm glad you've moved back here."

"Will you make those apple ebelskivers sometime?" he asked, sniffling as he cried into her chest. Celia's heart expanded with love for this boy, and he didn't even belong to her by blood. But he definitely belonged to her in some way.

"Tomorrow if you want," she said, stepping back and brushing the tears from his face. "Now, let's get this pie off your shoe. Your grandma won't like that in her wedding party."

Stockton stood and watched her clean it up, telling her about his school project. She got his shoe back on, and she hugged him again. "You should apologize to your dad."

"I know. I will." Stockton squeezed her tight and then left the bathroom. She sighed, one more trip to the laundry room in her future.

She caught sight of that charcoal-colored hat as she passed the living room entrance, and somehow, the cowboy felt the weight of her gaze, and their eyes met again. Something familiar struck her in the chest. She knew him....

"Time to line up," someone said, and Celia increased

her pace. Even though it only took a few seconds to get the cherry pie washcloth in the washing machine, by the time she returned to the hallway, it seemed everyone had a partner.

Except her.

Her breath caught in her throat, and she felt at a loss for what to do. This was a familiar feeling for Celia, as the moment Brandon had died, she'd been adrift with two small children. Everything became *except her*. Everyone had someone to sit by at church—except her. Everyone had a date on Valentine's Day—except her. Everyone had someone to watch their children for ladies night at the rec center—except her.

She'd had to figure things out as she went. Find babysitters. Sit by the pastor's wife. Make cakes and bacon bouquets for her and Reagan and Ruth on Valentine's Day.

As if Moses himself had arrived to part the Red Sea, the crowd shifted, showing her the cowboy in the charcoal-colored hat.

"Need a partner?" he asked, that delicious smile on his face. He took a couple steps past Beau and Lily, and a horrible realization hit her with the force of a ton of bricks.

She did know him.

Zach Zuckerman.

She sucked in a breath, the memories from her childhood rushing through her like river rapids.

"Zach," she hissed, an undeniable and inexplicable fury and dislike overcoming her.

He paused, cocked his head, and studied her. Not three seconds passed before he said, "Celia Abbott." His smile vanished, and he looked at her with the same disdain all Abbotts had for the Zuckermans.

Going back for as many generations as Celia could remember, the Abbotts and Zuckermans had been enemies. They still owned ranches across the road from one another in Coral Canyon, and the feud continued to this day.

Celia didn't even remember what it was about.

But she knew she couldn't date Zach Zuckerman. Period. The end.

"Go on," Graham said, nudging Zach to the front of the line. "You're the best man, Zach. Celia, you're with him. It's time to start."

Celia looked at Zach, wondering how in the world this had happened. How he'd gotten here, inside the lodge that had become a sanctuary for her. How she could possibly link her arm through his and smile, even for a moment. Even for Amanda.

"Celia," Graham hissed, and she realized Zach had moved and had his elbow cocked toward her.

Seeing no other choice, she put her arm in his and faced the front.

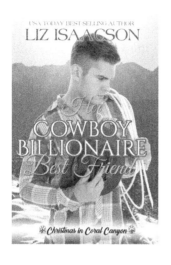

Her Cowboy Billionaire Best Friend (Book 1): Graham Whittaker returns to Coral Canyon a few days after Christmas—after the death of his father. He takes over the energy company his dad built from the ground up and buys a high-end lodge to live in—only a mile from the home of his once-best friend, Laney McAllister. They were best friends once, but Laney's always entertained feelings for him, and spending so much time with him while they make Christmas memories puts her heart in danger of getting broken again…

Her Cowboy Billionaire Boss (Book 2): Since the death of his wife a few years ago, Eli Whittaker has been running from one job to another, unable to find somewhere for him and his son to settle. Meg Palmer is Stockton's nanny, and she comes with her boss, Eli, to the lodge, her long-time crush on the man no different in Wyoming than it was on the beach. When she confesses her feelings for him and gets nothing in return, she's crushed, embarrassed, and unsure if she can stay in Coral Canyon for Christmas. Then Eli starts to show some feelings for her too…

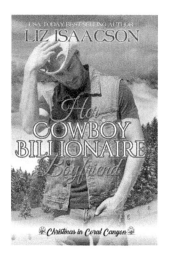

Her Cowboy Billionaire Boyfriend (Book 3): Andrew Whittaker is the public face for the Whittaker Brothers' family energy company, and with his older brother's robot about to be announced, he needs a press secretary to help him get everything ready and tour the state to make the announcements. When he's hit by a protest sign being carried by the company's biggest opponent, Rebecca Collings, he learns with a few clicks that she has the background they need. He offers her the job of press secretary when she thought she was going to be arrested, and not only because the spark between them in so hot Andrew can't see straight.

Can Becca and Andrew work together and keep their relationship a secret? Or will hearts break in this classic romance retelling reminiscent of *Two Weeks Notice*?

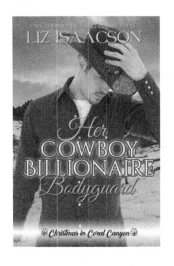

Her Cowboy Billionaire Bodyguard (Book 4): Beau Whittaker has watched his brothers find love one by one, but every attempt he's made has ended in disaster. Lily Everett has been in the spotlight since childhood and has half a dozen platinum records with her two sisters. She's taking a break from the brutal music industry and hiding out in Wyoming while her ex-husband continues to cause trouble for her. When she hears of Beau Whittaker and what he offers his clients, she wants to meet him. Beau is instantly attracted to Lily, but he tried a relationship with his last client that left a scar that still hasn't healed...

Can Lily use the spirit of Christmas to discover what matters most? Will Beau open his heart to the possibility of love with someone so different from him?

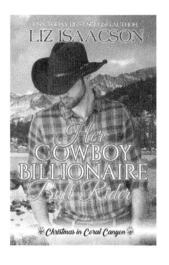

Her Cowboy Billionaire Bull Rider (Book 5): Todd Christopherson has just retired from the professional rodeo circuit and returned to his hometown of Coral Canyon. Problem is, he's got no family there anymore, no land, and no job. Not that he needs a job--he's got plenty of money from his illustrious career riding bulls.

Then Todd gets thrown during a routine horseback ride up the canyon, and his only support as he recovers physically is the beautiful Violet Everett. She's no nurse, but she does the best she can for the handsome cowboy. **Will she lose her heart to the billionaire bull rider? Can Todd trust that God led him to Coral Canyon...and Vi?**

Her Cowboy Billionaire Bachelor (Book 6): Rose Everett isn't sure what to do with her life now that her country music career is on hold. After all, with both of her sisters in Coral Canyon, and one about to have a baby, they're not making albums anymore.

Liam Murphy has been working for Doctors Without Borders, but he's back in the US now, and looking to start a new clinic in Coral Canyon, where he spent his summers.

When Rose wins a date with Liam in a bachelor auction, their relationship blooms and grows quickly. **Can Liam and Rose find a solution to their problems that doesn't involve one of them leaving Coral Canyon with a broken heart?**

Her Cowboy Billionaire Blind Date (Book 7): Her sons want her to be happy, but she's too old to be set up on a blind date...isn't she?

Amanda Whittaker has been looking for a second chance at love since the death of her husband several years ago. Finley Barber is a cowboy in every sense of the word. Born and raised on a racehorse farm in Kentucky, he's since moved to Dog Valley and started his own breeding stable for champion horses. He hasn't dated in years, and everything about Amanda makes him nervous.

Will Amanda take the leap of faith required to be with Finn? Or will he become just another boyfriend who doesn't make the cut?

Her Cowboy Billionaire Best Man (Book 8): When Celia Abbott-Armstrong runs into a gorgeous cowboy at her best friend's wedding, she decides she's ready to start dating again.

But the cowboy is Zach Zuckerman, and the Zuckermans and Abbotts have been at war for generations.

Can Zach and Celia find a way to reconcile their family's differences so they can have a future together?

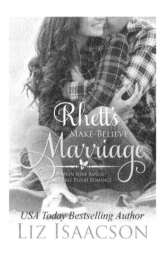

Rhett's Make-Believe Marriage (Book 1): She needs a husband to be credible as a matchmaker. He wants to help a neighbor. Will their fake marriage take them out of the friend zone?

Tripp's Trivial Tie (Book 2): She needs a husband to keep her son. He's wanted to take their relationship to the next level, but she's always pushing him away. Will their trivial tie take them all the way to happily-ever-after?

Liam's Invented I-Do (Book 3): She needs a husband to be credible as a matchmaker. He wants to help a neighbor. Will their fake marriage take them out of the friend zone?

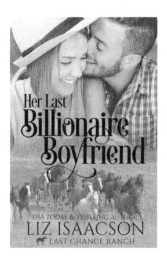

Her Last Billionaire Boyfriend (Book 2): A billionaire cowboy without a home meets a woman who secretly makes food videos to pay her debts...Can Carson and Adele do more than fight in the kitchens at Last Chance Ranch?

Her Last Make-Believe Marriage (Book 3): A female carpenter needs a husband just for a few days... Can Jeri and Sawyer navigate the minefield of a pretend marriage before their feelings become real?

Her Last Second Chance (Book 4): An Army cowboy, the woman he dated years ago, and their last chance at Last Chance Ranch... Can Dave and Sissy put aside hurt feelings and make their second chance romance work?

Her Last Secret Sweetheart (Book 5): A former dairy farmer and the marketing director on the ranch have to work together to make the cow cuddling program a success. But can Karla let Cache into her life? Or will she keep all her secrets from him - and keep *him* a secret too?

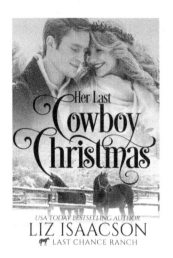

USA TODAY BESTSELLING AUTHOR
LIZ ISAACSON
LAST CHANCE RANCH

Her Last Cowboy Christmas (Book 6): She's tired of having her heart broken by cowboys. He waited too long to ask her out. Can Lance fix things quickly, or will Amber leave Last Chance Ranch before he can tell her how he feels?

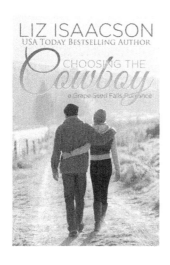

Choosing the Cowboy (Book 1): With financial trouble and personal issues around every corner, can Maggie Duffin and Chase Carver rely on their faith to find their happily-ever-after?

A spinoff from the #1 bestselling Three Rivers Ranch Romance novels, also by USA Today bestselling author Liz Isaacson.

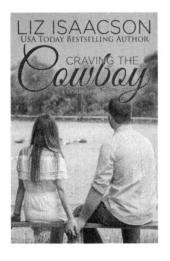

Craving the Cowboy (Book 2): Dwayne Carver is set to inherit his family's ranch in the heart of Texas Hill Country, and in order to keep up with his ranch duties and fulfill his dreams of owning a horse farm, he hires top trainer Felicity Lightburne. They get along great, and she can envision herself on this new farm—at least until her mother falls ill and she has to return to help her. Can Dwayne and Felicity work through their differences to find their happily-ever-after?

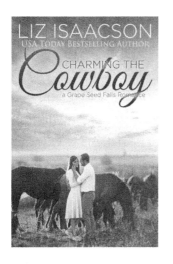

Charming the Cowboy (Book 3): Third grade teacher Heather Carver has had her eye on Levi Rhodes for a couple of years now, but he seems to be blind to her attempts to charm him. When she breaks her arm while on his horse ranch, Heather infiltrates Levi's life in ways he's never thought of, and his strict anti-female stance slips. Will Heather heal his emotional scars and he care for her physical ones so they can have a real relationship?

Courting the Cowboy (Book 4): Frustrated with the cowboy-only dating scene in Grape Seed Falls, May Sotheby joins TexasFaithful.com, hoping to find her soul mate without having to relocate--or deal with cowboy hats and boots. She has no idea that Kurt Pemberton, foreman at Grape Seed Ranch, is the man she starts communicating with... Will May be able to follow her heart and get Kurt to forgive her so they can be together?

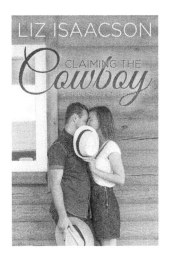

Claiming the Cowboy, Royal Brothers Book 1 (Grape Seed Falls Romance Book 5): Unwilling to be tied down, farrier Robin Cook has managed to pack her entire life into a two-hundred-and-eighty square-foot house, and that includes her Yorkie. Cowboy and co-foreman, Shane Royal has had his heart set on Robin for three years, even though she flat-out turned him down the last time he asked her to dinner. But she's back at Grape Seed Ranch for five weeks as she works her horse-shoeing magic, and he's still interested, despite a bitter life lesson that left a bad taste for marriage in his mouth.

Robin's interested in him too. But can she find room for Shane in her tiny house--and can he take a chance on her with his tired heart?

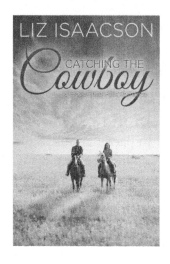

Catching the Cowboy, Royal Brothers Book 2 (Grape Seed Falls Romance Book 6): Dylan Royal is good at two things: whistling and caring for cattle. When his cows are being attacked by an unknown wild animal, he calls Texas Parks & Wildlife for help. He wasn't expecting a beautiful mammologist to show up, all flirty and fun and everything Dylan didn't know he wanted in his life.

Hazel Brewster has gone on more first dates than anyone in Grape Seed Falls, and she thinks maybe Dylan deserves a second... Can they find their way through wild animals, huge life changes, and their emotional pasts to find their forever future?

Cheering the Cowboy, Royal Brothers Book 3 (Grape Seed Falls Romance Book 7): Austin Royal loves his life on his new ranch with his brothers. But he doesn't love that Shayleigh Hatch came with the property, nor that he has to take the blame for the fact that he now owns her childhood ranch. They rarely have a conversation that doesn't leave him furious and frustrated--and yet he's still attracted to Shay in a strange, new way.

Shay inexplicably likes him too, which utterly confuses and angers her. As they work to make this Christmas the best the Triple Towers Ranch has ever seen, can they also navigate through their rocky relationship to smoother waters?

BOOKS IN THE STEEPLE RIDGE ROMANCE SERIES:

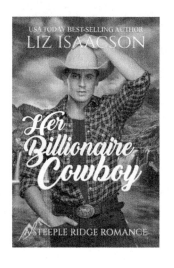

Her Billionaire Cowboy (Book 1): Tucker Jenkins has had enough of tall buildings, traffic, and has traded in his technology firm in New York City for Steeple Ridge Horse Farm in rural Vermont. Missy Marino has worked at the farm since she was a teen, and she's always dreamed of owning it. But her ex-husband left her with a truckload of debt, making her fantasies of owning the farm unfulfilled. Tucker didn't come to the country to find a new wife, but he supposes a woman could help him start over in Steeple Ridge. Will Tucker and Missy be able to navigate the shaky ground between them to find a new beginning?

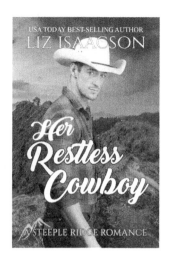

Her Restless Cowboy (Book 2): Ben Buttars is the youngest of the four Buttars brothers who come to Steeple Ridge Farm, and he finally feels like he's landed somewhere he can make a life for himself. Reagan Cantwell is a decade older than Ben and the recreational direction for the town of Island Park. Though Ben is young, he knows what he wants—and that's Rae. Can she figure out how to put what matters most in her life—family and faith —above her job before she loses Ben?

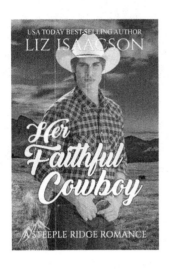

Her Faithful Cowboy (Book 3): Sam Buttars has spent the last decade making sure he and his brothers stay together. They've been at Steeple Ridge for a while now, but with the youngest married and happy, the siren's call to return to his parents' farm in Wyoming is loud in Sam's ears. He'd just go if it weren't for beautiful Bonnie Sherman, who roped his heart the first time he saw her. Do Sam and Bonnie have the faith to find comfort in each other instead of in the people who've already passed?

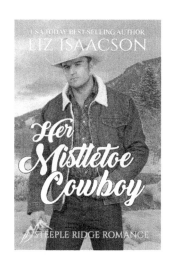

Her Mistletoe Cowboy (Book 4): Logan Buttars has always been good-natured and happy-go-lucky. After watching two of his brothers settle down, he recognizes a void in his life he didn't know about. Veterinarian Layla Guyman has appreciated Logan's friendship and easy way with animals when he comes into the clinic to get the service dogs. But with his future at Steeple Ridge in the balance, she's not sure a relationship with him is worth the risk. Can she rely on her faith and employ patience to tame Logan's wild heart?

Her Patient Cowboy (Book 5): Darren Buttars is cool, collected, and quiet—and utterly devastated when his girlfriend of nine months, Farrah Irvine, breaks up with him because he wanted her to ride her horse in a parade. But Farrah doesn't ride anymore, a fact she made very clear to Darren. She returned to her childhood home with so much baggage, she doesn't know where to start with the unpacking. Darren's the only Buttars brother who isn't married, and he wants to make Island Park his permanent home—with Farrah. Can they find their way through the heartache to achieve a happily-ever-after together?

Falling for Her Boss: A Horseshoe Home Ranch Romance (Book 1): Jace Lovell only has one thing left after his fiancé abandons him at the altar: his job at Horseshoe Home Ranch. Belle Edmunds is back in Gold Valley and she's desperate to build a portfolio that she can use to start her own firm in Montana. Jace isn't anywhere near forgiving his fiancé, and he's not sure he's ready for a new relationship with someone as fiery and beautiful as Belle. Can she employ her patience while he figures out how to forgive so they can find their own brand of happily-ever-after?

Falling for Her Roommate: A Horseshoe Home Ranch Romance (Book 2): Professional snowboarder Sterling Maughan has sequestered himself in his family's cabin in the exclusive mountain community above Gold Valley, Montana after a devastating fall that ended his career. Norah Watson cleans Sterling's cabin and the more time they spend together, the more Sterling is interested in all things Norah. As his body heals, so does his faith. Will Norah be able to trust Sterling so they can have a chance at true love?

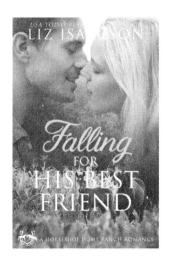

Falling for His Best Friend: A Horseshoe Home Ranch Romance (Book 3): Landon Edmunds has been a cowboy his whole life. An accident five years ago ended his successful rodeo career, and now he's looking to start a horse ranch-- and he's looking outside of Montana. Which would be great if God hadn't brought Megan Palmer back to Gold Valley right when Landon is looking to leave. Megan and Landon work together well, and as sparks fly, she's sure God brought her back to Gold Valley so she could find her happily ever after. Through serious discussion and prayer, can Landon and Megan find their future together?

Be sure to check out the spinoff series, the Brush Creek Brides romances after you read FALLING FOR HIS BEST FRIEND. Start with A WEDDING FOR THE WIDOWER.

Falling for His Nanny: A Horseshoe Home Ranch Romance (Book 4): Twelve years ago, Owen Carr left Gold Valley—and his long-time girlfriend—in favor of a country music career in Nashville. Married and divorced, Natalie teaches ballet at the dance studio in Gold Valley, but she never auditioned for the professional company the way she dreamed of doing. With Owen back, she realizes all the opportunities she missed out on when he left all those years ago—including a future with him. Can they mend broken bridges in order to have a second chance at love?

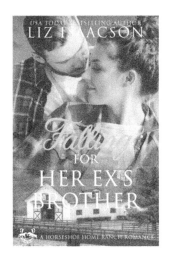

Falling for Her Ex's Brother: A Horseshoe Home Ranch Romance (Book 5): Caleb Chamberlain has spent the last five years recovering from a horrible breakup, his alcoholism that stemmed from it, and the car accident that left him hospitalized. He's finally on the right track in his life—until Holly Gray, his twin brother's ex-fiance mistakes him for Nathan. Holly's back in Gold Valley to get the required veterinarian hours to apply for her graduate program. When the herd at Horseshoe Home comes down with pneumonia, Caleb and Holly are forced to work together in close quarters. Holly's over Nathan, but she hasn't forgiven him—or the woman she believes broke up their relationship. Can Caleb and Holly navigate such a rough past to find their happily-ever-after?

Journey to Steeple Ridge Farm with Holly—and fall in love with the cowboys there in the Steeple Ridge Romance series! Start with STARTING OVER AT STEEPLE RIDGE.

Falling for Her Old Boyfriend: A Horseshoe Home Ranch Romance (Book 6): Ty Barker has been dancing through the last thirty years of his life--and he's suddenly realized he's alone. River Lee Whitely is back in Gold Valley with her two little girls after a divorce that's left deep scars. She has a job at Silver Creek that requires her to be able to ride a horse, and she nearly tramples Ty at her first lesson. That's just fine by him, because River Lee is the girl Ty has never gotten over. Ty realizes River Lee needs time to settle into her new job, her new home, her new life as a single parent, but going slow has never been his style. But for River Lee, can Ty take the necessary steps to keep her in his life?

Falling for His Next Door Neighbor: A Horseshoe Home Ranch Romance (Book 7): Archer Bailey has already lost one job to Emersyn Enders, so he deliberately doesn't tell her about the cowhand job up at Horseshoe Home Ranch. Emery's temporary job is ending, but her obligations to her physically disabled sister aren't. As Archer and Emery work together, its clear that the sparks flying between them aren't all from their friendly competition over a job. Will Emery and Archer be able to navigate the ranch, their close quarters, and their individual circumstances to find love this holiday season?

Falling for His Nurse: A Horseshoe Home Ranch Romance (Book 8): Cowboy Elliott Hawthorne has just lost his best friend and cabin mate to the worst thing imaginable —marriage. When his brother calls about an accident with their father, Elliott rushes down to Gold Valley from the ranch only to be met with the most beautiful woman he's ever seen. His father's new physical therapist, London Marsh, likes the handsome face and gentle spirit she sees in Elliott too. Can Elliott and London navigate difficult family situations to find a happily-ever-after?

LIZ ISAACSON

Second Chance Ranch: A Three Rivers Ranch Romance (Book 1): After his deployment, injured and discharged Major Squire Ackerman returns to Three Rivers Ranch, wanting to forgive Kelly for ignoring him a decade ago. He'd like to provide the stable life she needs, but with old wounds opening and a ranch on the brink of financial collapse, it will take patience and faith to make their second chance possible.

Third Time's the Charm: A Three Rivers Ranch Romance (Book 2): First Lieutenant Peter Marshall has a truckload of debt and no way to provide for a family, but Chelsea helps him see past all the obstacles, all the scars. With so many unknowns, can Pete and Chelsea develop the love, acceptance, and faith needed to find their happily ever after?

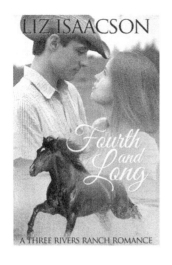

Fourth and Long: A Three Rivers Ranch Romance (Book 3): Commander Brett Murphy goes to Three Rivers Ranch to find some rest and relaxation with his Army buddies. Having his ex-wife show up with a seven-year-old she claims is his son is anything but the R&R he craves. Kate needs to make amends, and Brett needs to find forgiveness, but are they too late to find their happily ever after?

Fifth Generation Cowboy: A Three Rivers Ranch Romance (Book 4): Tom Lovell has watched his friends find their true happiness on Three Rivers Ranch, but everywhere he looks, he only sees friends. Rose Reyes has been bringing her daughter out to the ranch for equine therapy for months, but it doesn't seem to be working. Her challenges with Mari are just as frustrating as ever. Could Tom be exactly what Rose needs? Can he remove his friendship blinders and find love with someone who's been right in front of him all this time?

LIZ ISAACSON

A THREE RIVERS RANCH ROMANCE NOVELLA

Sixth Street Love Affair: A Three Rivers Ranch Romance (Book 5): After losing his wife a few years back, Garth Ahlstrom thinks he's ready for a second chance at love. But Juliette Thompson has a secret that could destroy their budding relationship. Can they find the strength, patience, and faith to make things work?

The Seventh Sergeant: A Three Rivers Ranch Romance (Book 6): Life has finally started to settle down for Sergeant Reese Sanders after his devastating injury overseas. Discharged from the Army and now with a good job at Courage Reins, he's finally found happiness—until a horrific fall puts him right back where he was years ago: Injured and depressed. Carly Watters, Reese's new veteran care coordinator, dislikes small towns almost as much as she loathes cowboys. But she finds herself faced with both when she gets assigned to Reese's case. Do they have the humility and faith to make their relationship more than professional?

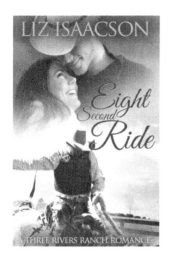

Eight Second Ride: A Three Rivers Ranch Romance (Book 7): Ethan Greene loves his work at Three Rivers Ranch, but he can't seem to find the right woman to settle down with. When sassy yet vulnerable Brynn Bowman shows up at the ranch to recruit him back to the rodeo circuit, he takes a different approach with the barrel racing champion. His patience and newfound faith pay off when a friendship--and more-- starts with Brynn. But she wants out of the rodeo circuit right when Ethan wants to rejoin. Can they find the path God wants them to take and still stay together?

The First Lady of Three Rivers Ranch: A Three Rivers Ranch Romance (Book 8): Heidi Duffin has been dreaming about opening her own bakery since she was thirteen years old. She scrimped and saved for years to afford baking and pastry school in San Francisco. And now she only has one year left before she's a certified pastry chef. Frank Ackerman's father has recently retired, and he's taken over the largest cattle ranch in the Texas Panhandle. A horseman through and through, he's also nearing thirty-one and looking for someone to bring love and joy to a homestead that's been dominated by men for a decade. But when he convinces Heidi to come clean the cowboy cabins, she changes all that. But the siren's call of a bakery is still loud in Heidi's ears, even if she's also seeing a future with Frank. Can she rely on her faith in ways she's never had to before or will their relationship end when summer does?

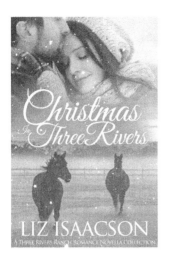

Christmas in Three Rivers: A Three Rivers Ranch Romance (Book 9): Isn't Christmas the best time to fall in love? The cowboys of Three Rivers Ranch think so. Join four of them as they journey toward their path to happily ever after in four, all-new novellas in the Amazon #1 Bestselling Three Rivers Ranch Romance series.

THE NINTH INNING: The Christmas season has never felt like such a burden to boutique owner Andrea Larsen. But with Mama gone and the holidays upon her, Andy finds herself wishing she hadn't been so quick to judge her former boyfriend, cowboy Lawrence Collins. Well, Lawrence hasn't forgotten about Andy either, and he devises a plan to get her out to the ranch so they can reconnect. Do they have the faith and humility to patch things up and start a new relationship?

TEN DAYS IN TOWN: Sandy Keller is tired of the dating scene in Three Rivers. Though she owns the pancake house, she's looking for a fresh start, which means an escape from the town where she grew up. When her older brother's best friend, Tad Jorgensen, comes to town for the holidays, it is a balm to his weary soul. A helicopter tour guide who experienced a near-death experience, he's looking to start over too--but in Three Rivers. Can Sandy and Tad navigate their troubles to find the path God wants them to take--and discover true love--in only ten days?

ELEVEN YEAR REUNION: Pastry chef extraordinaire, Grace Lewis has moved to Three Rivers to help Heidi Ackerman open a bakery in Three Rivers. Grace relishes the idea of starting over in a town where no one knows about her failed cupcakery. She doesn't expect to run into her old high school boyfriend, Jonathan Carver. A carpenter working at Three Rivers Ranch, Jon's in town against his will. But with Grace now on the scene, Jon's thinking life in Three Rivers is suddenly looking up. But with her focus on baking and his disdain for small towns, can they make their eleven year reunion stick?

THE TWELFTH TOWN: Newscaster Taryn Tucker has had enough of life on-screen. She's bounced from town to town before arriving in Three Rivers, completely alone and completely anonymous--just the way she now likes it. She takes a job cleaning at Three Rivers Ranch, hoping for a chance to figure out who she is and where God wants her. When she meets happy-go-lucky cowhand Kenny Stockton, she doesn't expect sparks to fly. Kenny's always been "the best friend" for his female friends, but the pull between him and Taryn can't be denied. Will they have the courage and faith necessary to make their opposite worlds mesh?

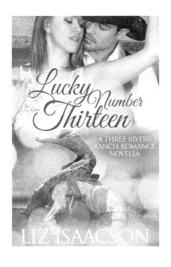

Lucky Number Thirteen: A Three Rivers Ranch Romance (Book 10): Tanner Wolf, a rodeo champion ten times over, is excited to be riding in Three Rivers for the first time since he left his philandering ways and found religion. Seeing his old friends Ethan and Brynn is therapuetic--until a terrible accident lands him in the hospital. With his rodeo career over, Tanner thinks maybe he'll stay in town--and it's not just because his nurse, Summer Hamblin, is the prettiest woman he's ever met. But Summer's the queen of first dates, and as she looks for a way to make a relationship with the transient rodeo star work Summer's not sure she has the fortitude to go on a second date. Can they find love among the tragedy?

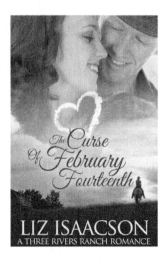

The Curse of February Fourteenth: A Three Rivers Ranch Romance (Book 11): Cal Hodgkins, cowboy veterinarian at Bowman's Breeds, isn't planning to meet anyone at the masked dance in small-town Three Rivers. He just wants to get his bachelor friends off his back and sit on the sidelines to drink his punch. But when he sees a woman dressed in gorgeous butterfly wings and cowgirl boots with blue stitching, he's smitten. Too bad she runs away from the dance before he can get her name, leaving only her boot behind...

Fifteen Minutes of Fame: A Three Rivers Ranch Romance (Book 12): Navy Richards is thirty-five years of tired—tired of dating the same men, working a demanding job, and getting her heart broken over and over again. Her aunt has always spoken highly of the matchmaker in Three Rivers, Texas, so she takes a six-month sabbatical from her high-stress job as a pediatric nurse, hops on a bus, and meets with the matchmaker. Then she meets Gavin Redd. He's handsome, he's hardworking, and he's a cowboy. But is he an Aquarius too? Navy's not making a move until she knows for sure...

Sixteen Steps to Fall in Love: A Three Rivers Ranch Romance (Book 13): A chance encounter at a dog park sheds new light on the tall, talented Boone that Nicole can't ignore. As they get to know each other better and start to dig into each other's past, Nicole is the one who wants to run. This time from her growing admiration and attachment to Boone. From her aging parents. From herself.

But Boone feels the attraction between them too, and he decides he's tired of running and ready to make Three Rivers his permanent home. **Can Boone and Nicole use their faith to overcome their differences and find a happily-ever-after together?**

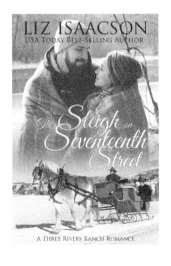

The Sleigh on Seventeenth Street: A Three Rivers Ranch Romance (Book 14): A cowboy with skills as an electrician tries a relationship with a down-on-her luck plumber. Can Dylan and Camila make water and electricity play nicely together this Christmas season? Or will they get shocked as they try to make their relationship work?

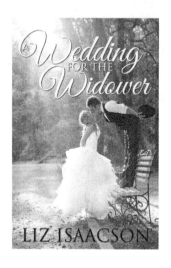

A Wedding for the Widower: Brush Creek Brides Romance (Book 1): Former rodeo champion and cowboy Walker Thompson trains horses at Brush Creek Horse Ranch, where he lives a simple life in his cabin with his ten-year-old son. A widower of six years, he's worked with Tess Wagner, a widow who came to Brush Creek to escape the turmoil of her life to give her seven-year-old son a slower pace of life. But Tess's breast cancer is back...

Walker will have to decide if he'd rather spend even a short time with Tess than not have her in his life at all. Tess wants to feel God's love and power, but can she discover and accept God's will in order to find her happy ending?

A Companion for the Cowboy: Brush Creek Brides Romance (Book 2): Cowboy and professional roper Justin Jackman has found solitude at Brush Creek Horse Ranch, preferring his time with the animals he trains over dating. With two failed engagements in his past, he's not really interested in getting his heart  stomped on again. But when flirty and fun Renee Martin picks him up at a church ice cream bar--on a bet, no less-- he finds himself more than just a little interested. His Gen-X attitudes are attractive to her; her Millennial behaviors drive him nuts. Can Justin look past their differences and take a chance on another engagement?

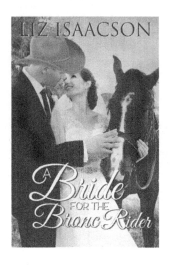

A Bride for the Bronc Rider: Brush Creek Brides Romance (Book 3): Ted Caldwell has been a retired bronc rider for years, and he thought he was perfectly happy training horses to buck at Brush Creek Ranch. He was wrong. When he meets April Nox, who comes to the ranch to hide her pregnancy from all her friends back in Jackson Hole, Ted realizes he has a huge family-shaped hole in his life. April is embarrassed, heartbroken, and trying to find her extinguished faith. She's never ridden a horse and wants nothing to do with a cowboy ever again. Can Ted and April create a family of happiness and love from a tragedy?

A Family for the Farmer: Brush Creek Brides Romance (Book 4): Blake Gibbons oversees all the agriculture at Brush Creek Horse Ranch, sometimes moonlighting as a general contractor. When he meets Erin Shields, new in town, at her aunt's bakery, he's instantly smitten. Erin moved to Brush Creek after a divorce that left 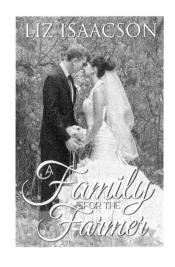 her penniless, homeless, and a single mother of three children under age eight. She's nowhere near ready to start dating again, but the longer Blake hangs around the bakery, the more she starts to like him. Can Blake and Erin find a way to blend their lifestyles and become a family?

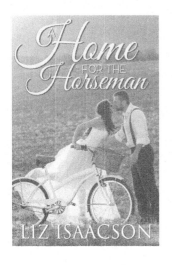

A Home for the Horseman: Brush Creek Brides Romance (Book 5): Emmett Graves has always had a positive outlook on life. He adores training horses to become barrel racing champions during the day and cuddling with his cat at night. Fresh off her professional rodeo retirement, Molly Brady comes to Brush Creek Horse Ranch as Emmett's protege. He's not thrilled, and she's allergic to cats. Oh, and she'd like to stay cowboy-free, thank you very much. But Emmett's about as cowboy as they come.... Can Emmett and Molly work together without falling in love?

A Refuge for the Rancher: Brush Creek Brides Romance (Book 6): Grant Ford spends his days training cattle—when he's not camped out at the elementary school hoping to catch a glimpse of his ex-girl-friend. When principal Shannon Sharpe confronts him and asks him to stay away from the school, the spark between

them is instant and hot. Shannon's expecting a transfer very soon, but she also needs a summer outdoor coordinator—and Grant fits the bill. Just because he's handsome and everything Shannon's ever wanted in a cowboy husband means nothing. Will Grant and Shannon be able to survive the summer or will the Utah heat be too much for them to handle?

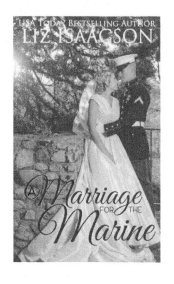

A Marriage for the Marine: A Fuller Family Novel - Brush Creek Brides Romance (Book 7): Tate Benson can't believe he's come to Nowhere, Utah, to fix up a house that hasn't been inhabited in years. But he has. Because he's retired from the Marines and looking to start a life as a police officer in small-town Brush Creek. Wren Fuller has her hands full most days running her family's company. When Tate calls and demands a maid for that morning, she decides to have the calls forwarded to her cell and go help him out. She didn't know he was moving in next door, and she's completely unprepared for his handsomeness, his kind heart, and his wounded soul.Can Tate and Wren weather a relationship when they're also next-door neighbors?

A Fiancé for the Firefighter: A Fuller Family Novel - Brush Creek Brides Romance (Book 8): Cora Wesley comes to Brush Creek, hoping to get some in-the-wild firefighting training as she prepares to put in her application to be a hotshot. When she meets Brennan Fuller, the spark between them is hot and instant. As they get to know

each other, her deadline is constantly looming over them, and Brennan starts to wonder if he can break ranks in the family business. He's okay mowing lawns and hanging out with his brothers, but he dreams of being able to go to college and become a landscape architect, but he's just not sure it can be done. Will Cora and Brennan be able to endure their trials to find true love?

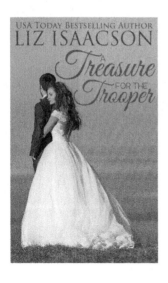

A Treasure for the Trooper: A Fuller Family Novel - Brush Creek Brides Romance (Book 9): Dawn Fuller has made some mistakes in her life, and she's not proud of the way McDermott Boyd found her off the road one day last year. She's spent a hard year wrestling with her choices and trying to fix them, glad for McDermott's acceptance and friendship. He lost his wife years ago, done his best with his daughter, and now he's ready to move on. Can McDermott help Dawn find a way past her former mistakes and down a path that leads to love, family, and happiness?

A Date for the Detective: A Fuller Family Novel - Brush Creek Brides Romance (Book 10): Dahlia Reid is one of the best detectives Brush Creek and the surrounding towns has ever had. She's given up on the idea of marriage—and pleasing her mother—and has dedicated herself fully to her job. Which is great, since one of the most perplexing cases of her career

has come to town. Kyler Fuller thinks he's finally ready to move past the woman who ghosted him years ago. He's cut his hair, and he's ready to start dating. Too bad every woman he's been out with is about as interesting as a lamppost—until Dahlia. He finds her beautiful, her quick wit a breath of fresh air, and her intelligence sexy. Can Kyler and Dahlia use their faith to find a way through the obstacles threatening to keep them apart?

A Partner for the Paramedic: A Fuller Family Novel - Brush Creek Brides Romance (Book 11): Jazzy Fuller has always been overshadowed by her prettier, more popular twin, Fabiana. Fabi meets paramedic Max Robinson at the park and sets a date with him only to come down with the flu. So she convinces Jazzy to cut her hair and take her place on the date. And the spark between Jazzy and Max is hot and instant...if only he knew she wasn't her sister, Fabi.

Max drives the ambulance for the town of Brush Creek with is partner Ed Moon, and neither of them have been all that lucky in love. Until Max suggests to who he thinks is Fabi that they should double with Ed and Jazzy. They do, and Fabi is smitten with the steady, strong Ed Moon. As each twin falls further and further in love with their respective paramedic, it becomes obvious they'll need to come clean about the switcheroo sooner rather than later...or risk losing their hearts.

A Catch for the Chief: A Fuller Family Novel - Brush Creek Brides Romance (Book 12): Berlin Fuller has struck out with the dating scene in Brush Creek more times than she cares to admit. When she makes a deal with her friends that they can choose the next man she goes out with, she didn't dream they'd pick surly Cole Fairbanks, the new Chief of Police.

His friends call him the Beast and challenge him to complete ten dates that summer or give up his bonus check. When Berlin approaches him, stuttering about the deal with her friends and claiming they don't actually have to go out, he's intrigued. As the summer passes, Cole finds himself burning both ends of the candle to keep up with his job and his new relationship. When he unleashes the Beast one time too many, Berlin will have to decide if she can tame him or if she should walk away.

ABOUT LIZ

Liz Isaacson writes inspirational romance, usually set in Texas, or Montana, or anywhere else horses and cowboys exist. She lives in Utah, where she teaches elementary school, taxis her daughter to dance several times a week, and eats a lot of Ferrero Rocher while writing. Find her on her website at lizisaacson.com.

Made in the USA
Monee, IL
02 May 2021